Spiral of Lies
A Johnny One Eye Novel

David Stuart Davies

This edition published in 2019 by Sharpe Books.

'Foul deeds will rise,
Though all the earth o'erwhelm them, to men's eyes'
Hamlet

CONTENTS

PROLOGUE

LONDON 1950

Emily Johnson enjoyed her job. It gave her pleasure every day – or to be more precise, every night. She was only a cleaner but she took pride in her work, and the fact that she cleaned the prestige offices on floor six gave her particular pride. She had passed the rigorous screening process and knew she was trusted with this special responsibility. She took charge of her domain, as she regarded it, after all the worker ants had left for the day. She loved moving through the empty, dimly lighted offices with her dusters, pail and mop. She loved the smell of the lavender polish as it permeated the air and the sense of order she brought the untidiness of the offices. She was the sole occupant of this silent world. For a break, she could sit at one of those posh oak desks, uncork her vacuum flask and take her tea imagining she was some important person making major decisions. She would tut-tut at over-filled ashtrays and half-eaten apples left on work surfaces, although the wastepaper bins were easy to deal with as all the paper contents had been shredded into thin spaghetti-like strips.

Occasionally one or two of the workers would stay on an extra hour after the official finishing time to complete some urgent job and this irritated her as it upset her set routine. She regarded them as intruders who were usurping her role as mistress of all she surveyed. She had to wait until they eventually departed, causing her to interrupt her regimented routine. So it was on Wednesday 13th of September. She spotted a light on in Room 4C. With a grunt of irritation, she tapped on the door. She had to ascertain if there was someone still in there or if the light had been left on accidentally.

There was a long pause without a reply, but she could hear some kind of activity taking place inside. She coughed loudly and tapped again with more gusto, adding a gentle 'Hello there…?'

Eventually, the door was opened by a well-built man in his shirt sleeves. His face bore an expression which Emily Johnson thought was a mixture of irritation and apprehension. The eyes

1

had a certain wild look about them. It was a face that Emily had not seen before.

'Yes, what do you want?' he snapped, his voice somewhat hoarse as though it hadn't been used for some time.

'Cleaner, sir,' she said. 'Just checking about the light. There's usually nobody about at this time of night. All gone home, like.'

The man's features relaxed somewhat and he even managed a tight little smile.

'Ah, yes. I'm... I'm nearly ready to go myself. Just a few last things to do. Another fifteen minutes and I'll be out of your hair.'

'Ooh, that's all right, sir. I just wanted to check. I can do this office last.'

'Fine,' he said and closed the door.

She didn't see him leave. She didn't see him carry with him a small attaché case and even if she had, she wouldn't have realised that amongst other things, it contained a very small camera.

A man, whom many knew only by the name Socrates, entered a small office in one of the buildings in a narrow street near Whitehall. Two other men were already in the office seated at a small rectangular table. They could almost have been twins. Both had undernourished features, thin gaunt faces, dark hair slicked back with hair oil and each wore matching black suits, white shirts and plain grey ties. They obviously had been awaiting the arrival of Socrates. He gave them a silent nod of acknowledgement as he took a chair at the head of the table. He was a handsome man in his late fifties with a passing resemblance to the film star Ronald Colman. On this occasion his face was stern and the bright blue eyes held a hard glitter. He leaned forward, his hands splaying out onto the table. 'Well, gentlemen, he's made his move at last and a pretty serious move it is, too. Now it's time for us to take action.'

The two men nodded in unison.

'He intends to make the transfer today. The usual spot, no doubt. You must stop him'.

The pair exchanged guarded looks. 'Leave it to us, sir,' said the one with the moustache, which made him look slightly older although both men were the same age.

'Good,' said Socrates, 'This is important. You must not fail.'

CHAPTER ONE

He woke early. As usual. Something intangible always roused him from his unsettling dreams at this time of day. It came most mornings as dawn was breaking and the early light attempted to squeeze its way through the gaps in the bedroom curtains. He surfaced and felt tense, frightened. It usually was some irrational fear that caused this unease. He was aware of that and usually managed to convince himself that there really was nothing to worry about. But today he failed because he knew that this morning he had a very sound tangible reason to be fearful. He lay, flat on his back, his body damp with sweat, staring at the ceiling, his whole being trembling with apprehension.

He acknowledged that it was the price he had to pay for the man he had become and the risky route through life that he had chosen to take. It was the cliff edge path and it only needed a strong errant wind to blow him over into oblivion on to the rocks below.

He reached out to the bedside table and retrieved a pack of cigarettes and a lighter. Pulling himself up into a sitting position, he lit up. The tobacco had a calming effect on him and the dark irrationalities of the night began to fade, but the realities of the day ahead stayed, causing his head to ache. The woman at his side stirred in her sleep and shifted her position. He gazed down at her pale features. She was pretty and he was fond of her. It was a fondness that did not quite stretch to love but he accepted that without dismay. He valued her companionship and as a sexual partner, but he was fairly certain that he did not have the capacity to surrender his emotions to the romantic concept of love. He was too selfish and too concerned with self-preservation to allow such feelings to invade his sensibilities. Love could damage and destroy and he was having none of it. Nevertheless, he leaned forward and kissed her forehead. She sighed dreamily, still not surfacing from her slumbers.

Another cigarette and he turned his thoughts to today's mission. It should be simple and rewarding, but he was well aware that there were great risks involved and it was fraught with dangerous possibilities. He ran through the scenario in his mind, imagining it like a film with himself as both the audience and the central character. The scenario ran smoothly as it should – as he hoped it would in reality. He could do no more now.

Dragging himself from the bed, he moved to the window and parted the curtains to gaze out. Well, it looked like it would turn out to be a nice fine day. Perhaps that was a good omen.

When he arrived at Russell Square Gardens at eleven that morning, it was indeed a nice fine day: a bright September sun blazed down from a cloudless sky and there were many folk there taking advantage of the late summer warmth, sitting on benches, lazing on the grass or strolling aimlessly around the gardens. He checked his watch. He was ten minutes early – as he had intended to be. He wandered around in what appeared a casual fashion but, his eyes were darting everywhere, alert and suspicious. He was well aware that once this deed was done there really was no going back. The titbits that he had supplied previously had satisfied his new masters up to a point but they had pressed him for more and offered more in return. Was it greed or some innate desire to feel that he was really involved in the new world and not just a bloody tin pot clerk that made him do what he did? Who could say? Well, certainly *he* didn't want to say. Probably because he knew he would have to plump for greed. He wrinkled his nose. So what? There was nothing wrong with that.

At length, he took a seat on a bench at the centre of the garden, near the fountain. The designated one. As he expected, the only other occupant was an old lady in a droopy grey coat and an ancient beret. She had brought a bag of birdseed with her and was busily scattering it for the pigeons which gathered around her. Laying his folded copy of *The Times* down on the bench, he lit a cigarette and took in his surroundings: the shifting panorama of London folk under an amber sun seemed to relax him.

The old lady surreptitiously inched along the bench closer to him, her voluminous coat spilling over to almost cover his copy of the newspaper.

'There you go, dearie,' he found himself saying – not a rehearsed response, but he was so relieved that, as far as he was concerned, his part of the deal was almost over. He was just about to leave when he noticed the woman stiffen and emit a strange, muted gasp. He turned to look at her. She was frozen as though petrified, her eyes staring into the distance, her lips quivering with fear. He followed her gaze and saw that it was focused on two men hurrying in the direction of the bench, each one dressed identically in fawn raincoats and bowler hats.

'Scarper,' rasped the woman. 'The game's up.'

He did not need further persuasion. Snatching up the copy of the *Times* he took to his heel, racing through the crowds, heading for the exit at the left-hand corner of the gardens. At one point he turned and saw one of the bowler-hatted men drag the old woman to her feet. She resisted and fell to the ground. As the man leaned over her, a shot rang out and her assailant flew backwards with a sharp cry of pain. Within seconds the woman was on her feet and in flight. It was quite clear that this was not an old woman at all. She raced through the throng of surprised onlookers like a speedy Olympian. Meanwhile, a small group gathered around the prone man.

Shocked by what he had seen, he thrust his way through the meandering crowd toward the exit to the gardens. As he did so, his pace faltered as he spotted a burly constable standing sentry by the gateway. He swivelled around and saw that the other bowler-hatted man was on his track, speeding in his direction. Out of desperation, he ran sideways, knocking over a small child who screamed in protest, as did his mother. Ignoring their cries, he left the path, skimmed over the flower beds and raced for the privet hedge at the bottom of the gardens. He had neither the time nor the inclination to turn round to see if his pursuer was hot on his tracks. He forced his way through the privet hedge, the spiny branches clinging to his coat and scratching his face. He burst on to the pavement to the surprise of several pedestrians and without hesitation sped down Russell Street, hoping to get lost in the crowd. Reaching the corner, he allowed himself a brief pause to cast a look back to see if he could see the bowler-hatted man. To his great relief, there was no sign of him. He heaved a sigh. With luck, he had shaken the blighter off.

His heart was thumping and his mind was a whirl and fearful, more fearful than it had ever been. The words of the 'old lady' came back to him: 'The game's up.'

The game's up.

My God! That meant he was off the cliff path.

The implication of this struck home so forcibly that he felt weak at the knees. In an instant, his world had crumbled. Now he was a fugitive. Now he was on the run. And so in order to survive, he had to keep moving.

Turning the corner, he saw the iron railings of the British Museum. He would take refuge here for a while to give himself time to work out what the hell he was going to do next.

CHAPTER TWO
From the Jotrnal of Johnny Hawke

I opened the bathroom window to allow the steam to escape after my morning clean-up campaign. I stared out over the familiar vista on my particular patch of the London skyline. The rooftops were shimmering with dewy dampness and an array of drunken chimney pots were sending up feeble columns of smoke into the slate grey of a September sky. There was the faint drone of traffic noise, as though the beast of the city was purring gently and rousing itself for a new day. A determined autumn sun was trying to break through, its burnt orange face just visible behind the dull murk. It would make it by noon, I reckoned. We were in for a pleasant day.

How long, I wondered, had I been looking out at this scene in all its seasons and moods. I did a quick mental calculation: ten years, ever since I started renting this particular corner of Christopher Court at the top end of the Tottenham Court Road, where I lived and had my office as 'John Hawke, Private Investigator'. Despite the various ravages of time, I was still here, still hanging on. I had survived the war, the death of close friends, and the loss of women I had loved. I had endured the fluctuating demands on my professional services, dining *à la carte* on some days, nibbling a few digestive biscuits washed down with tap water on others. Indeed, much good all my efforts have done me. I have hardly improved my lot in the world but at least I am a survivor - a lone survivor with little more to my name than when I first entered these premises that ocean of time ago. With this glum, negative thought, I closed the window, snapping the catch sharply.

Instinctively, I moved to the bathroom mirror and, with the edge of the towel draped around my neck, I wiped away the condensation and my ugly mug appeared there as though by magic. My thirty-seven-year-old ugly mug, to be precise. It was a little more lined than it had been when I first used this mirror to aid my shaving in 1940, and the hair was now flecked with grey, but the chin was still firm and sleek. Rationing had aided me in keeping my features from bloating and my stomach from expanding. Really, it was not a bad face apart from that blessed ugly eye patch which stuck out like a… well, like a blessed ugly eye patch. It was so much a part of me now and yet it still seemed like some monstrous dark blemish blighting my face. As this thought entered my head, I dismissed it immediately. I had no reason to feel sorry for myself; there were hundreds of ex-servicemen in this city in a far worse state than me. It was not only eyes that had been lost, but limbs, arms, legs and minds. Whole faces, bodies, brains and families had been ravaged by the senseless cruelty of war. And these men had received their injuries fighting for their country, while I lost my eye in a bloody farcical accident. It must have looked like a scene from a Chaplin movie: a novice soldier in training on the rifle range when…whoof, the rifle backfires and the novice squaddie loses both an eye and his career as a fighting soldier. Johnny One-Eye was born.

This sad, self-indulgent and oft repeated reverie was interrupted by a sharp rat a tat on the door of the bathroom, accompanied by a stern cry. 'You done in there, Mr Hawke? There are others who want to have a wash, you know.'

It was Mr Abrahams, a newly arrived ant in our little nest and he had not got used to my lengthy ablutions in the morning. Other inhabitants in the building had given up complaining about the time I spent bathing and shaving. They had learned to work around me, but Mr Abrahams was proving persistent. He was right, of course. I did spend too much time in the bathroom in the mornings. It was my psychological tic for delaying having to cope with the business of the day. While I scraped the stubble from my chin or wallowed in the tepid water of the great white tank that masqueraded as a bathtub, I was in a kind of peaceful limbo, the worries, traumas, demands of the day were held at bay. Once I exited this steamy haven I had to be grown up about things and face the slings and arrows of outrageous reality.

'I'll be out in a trice,' I cried, struggling into my bathrobe.

'A trice! What's that in English?' came the sarcastic reply.

I shrugged and grinned. I liked the old guy. He often made me

9

smile with his acerbic comments.

'Two minutes,' I said and began packing up my toilet bag. One of these days I'll have my own bathroom, I thought, as I did most mornings. It was a lovely dream, which I knew in my heart of hearts would never come true. But what is life without dreams, however futile and fragile?

With some alacrity, I returned to my office and the back room which I use as my living quarters. By the time I had dressed and wolfed down a couple of slices of toast thinly smeared with margarine, the big hand on my cheap pawnshop watch was moving towards nine. Nearly time to be on parade. I had an appointment with a client at nine-fifteen. It was with a Mrs Frances Clements. She had rung me the previous afternoon saying she needed my help desperately and could she call round that evening. I put her off until this morning. I had a ticket to see the Crazy Gang at the Palladium that night and I wasn't about to miss the show. I needed a few laughs and I knew they would provide them. Besides I had a long experience of ladies ringing me wanting my help 'desperately', only to discover that they were concerned about a missing pet, a lost raffle ticket or they imagined they were being followed by a tall dark stranger which turned out to be a wish fulfilment scenario fuelled by some screen romance they had seen at the local cinema. Trivia. In fact, now the war was over, it seemed that most of my cases dealt with trivia: petty thefts, sordid cases of adultery and lost relatives. I had little hope that Mrs Frances Clements would bring me a case which would prove challenging, exciting and put me on my detective mettle.

How wrong I was.

At nine-fifteen precisely – at least, according to the afore-mentioned cheap pawnshop watch – there was a ring at my office door and Mrs Clements entered. I had not really known what to expect. Her voice on the phone suggested a respectable middle-aged woman who was used to getting her own way. I suppose I was expecting a stoutish female in her forties, in a tight-fitting costume with probably a fox fur draped around her neck.

My deductions were completely awry.

Standing before me was a shapely creature, in her early thirties, I would guess. She wore little makeup – her fresh attractive features didn't need it – with her blonde hair cut in a neat attractive bob. She wore a dark red dress which followed the contours of her body beautifully and a smart woollen jacket. I have to admit that on seeing her, the old Hawke ticker skipped a beat. She certainly was a looker. She had wonderfully smooth, pale skin, with softly moulded features. There was a mole or beauty spot on her right cheek which actually enhanced her beauty. However, it only took a moment for me to throw a thick veil over my carnal inclinations and slip into professional mode. I offered the lady a seat and a cigarette. She accepted both. As she extracted the cigarette from my case, I noticed a large diamond ring on her finger. It was shaped like a snake, the gold band feathered like scales with the glittering stone in place of the reptile's head. This lady had money.

When we were both lit up and casting a fine grey mist into my cramped office, I asked her, 'How do you think I can help you?'

'By finding my husband,' she replied. Her voice was cool and controlled but nevertheless, there was air a faint air of emotion in her delivery.

'He has disappeared?'

She nodded and took a drag on her cigarette before continuing. 'He's been gone for about a week now.'

'That's a while. You'd better give me the full details.'

'His name is Walter Clements. He is thirty-five, well built with dark brown hair. About five foot eight. He works as a salesman for Klenco, the washing machine manufacturers. We've been married for two years.'

'Happily?'

'I thought so. I wasn't aware of any problems.'

I pursed my lips. Perhaps there was more to this declaration that met my one eye, but I let it lie for the moment. 'When you say he disappeared – how?'

'Well, he didn't come home from work last Wednesday. He was usually regular as clockwork. That was unless he was on a sales trip to another part of the country - his patch was the south-east of England – and then he would ring me every evening.'

11

'Was he away a great deal?'

'About four of five days every month, but he would tell me about his trips in advance. But he didn't on this occasion. The last words he spoke to me as he left that morning were, "See you tonight. I fancy sausages and mash for dinner if you can manage it."'

'Did you manage it?'

Mrs Clement frowned at my query and looked to be on the verge of chastising me for what she obviously regarded as a trivial remark, but instead, she just nodded. 'Yes, I did.'

'And Walter didn't come home.'

'No.' Her voice was querulous now. At this early stage of our relationship, I couldn't work out if she was genuinely upset or putting on a pretty convincing performance.

'Had he ever done this before?'

'Never. He was a meticulous timekeeper. I suppose he had to be with his job, keeping a number of appointments in a day.'

'Selling washing machines.'

'He wasn't a door to door salesman,' she snapped. 'He dealt with companies, institutions and laundries rather than domestic customers. The company thought very highly of him.'

I nodded sympathetically. 'Have you been to the police about his disappearance?'

Now the lady looked nervous and she hesitated, stubbing out her cigarette to cover her unease. 'No, I haven't been to the police…'

'Now that strikes me as odd,' I said, gently. 'Why not?'

'Because of this note.' She opened her handbag and withdrew a sheet of blue notepaper and passed to me. There was a short message in neat handwriting:

'I have to go away for a while. Don't worry. I am fine. Carry on as normal and do not go to the police. All will be well. W.'

'Is this your husband's handwriting?'

'Yes, yes, I think so.'

'You think so? You're not sure?'

'Well, yes I am.' She affirmed but I was not convinced.

'How did you receive this note?'

'I found it on the mat in the hall the morning after Walter

didn't come home. Someone… he must have pushed the note through the letterbox.'

'But why? Why didn't he come to give you the message in person?'

'I don't know. I don't know.' She shook her head vigorously and now the tears came, gentle, refined and, I thought, genuine. She fumbled in her handbag for a handkerchief and dabbed her eyes. I waited quietly. 'I'm sorry,' she said at length, giving her eyes a final gentle pat before returning the dampened hankie to her bag.

'It is understandable that you are upset,' I said. 'The situation must be most stressful. So you obeyed the instructions in the note but then after a week without any further news you thought you'd try a private investigator.'

She nodded. 'Yes.'

'Have you any notion why your husband would ask you not to go to the police? It seems an odd request.'

'I've no idea.'

'Has he even been in trouble with the law?'

'Certainly not,' she said, the fire returning to her demeanour. 'My husband is a decent and respectable man. I just need to know… I would like you to try and find out where he is and what has happened to him.'

Once more, I was being requested to produce the rabbit from the hat.

'Have you any idea at all where your husband might be? Or why he felt the need to disappear?'

'No. I wish I did. Don't you think I've wracked my brains to try and think of a reason – to try and explain this mystery?'

'You sure he's not involved with another woman?'

'A week ago I would have said definitely no, but all sorts of doubts creep in. I've no evidence to suggest he's been unfaithful.'

'Does he gamble or drink?'

'He does the pools and has a pint or two at the weekend, but nothing to excess.'

'What about his friends? Have you asked any of them if they know anything?'

'Well, Walter doesn't really have any friends. He's a very quiet, solitary man. We're just happy together, that's all.'

I wondered if this so-called happiness was an illusion, but kept that thought to myself for the moment. However, I knew that a happy man did not desert his wife without a very good reason. I reckoned old Walter boy was in some kind of hot water, probably of the scalding variety.

'Does he own a passport?' I asked.

'Yes, but he didn't take it with him.'

'Family?'

'His parents are dead. He has a sister who lives in America. She married a G. I.'

I groaned inwardly. This lady was not giving me very much to go on. Well, to be brutally frank, she was giving me nothing at all. I wandered to the window, pulled back the shabby net curtain and looked out on the alley beyond. *Time I came on strong*, I thought.

I turned suddenly to face Mrs Frances Clements. 'OK, lady,' I snarled, 'let's dispense with this pile of garbage you've dumped on my doorstep. Let's hear the truth. What really happened to drive your little hubby away? Why did he leave you and where do you think he is?'

This was my usual dramatic turn performed for clients who came with vague tales that usually contained as many holes as a giant colander. And more often than not it produced dividends, with the client taken aback by my sudden brutal behaviour and, crumbling under its unexpected ferocity, began filling in some of the crucial missing pieces in their story.

But not so on this occasion.

For a moment, Frances Clements stared open-mouthed in disbelief at me and then her eyes flashed with anger. She rose to her feet, scraping the chair back on the floorboard. She flung her arm out towards me in an accusatory fashion.

'How dare you, you bastard?' she cried with venom. 'I told you the truth. Do you think I'd come to a crummy detective agency If I knew where my husband was or had an inkling what had happened to him? You worm. Some detective you are.'

She turned abruptly and headed for the door.

'Whoa, lady, I'm sorry,' I called after her. 'I was just testing you, that's all. I had to be sure you were giving me your story straight. If I'm going to find your husband, I need to have the absolute truth. Please come back and sit down.'

She turned to face me, her features still taut with anger.

I held out my hand indicating the chair, adding gently, 'I'll do my best to find him.'

She glared at me for a time and then gave a sigh of resignation and, with some reluctance, resumed her seat. This lady was, I thought, on the level.

In a calm, business-like fashion I made a note of her address, phone number and the address of Klenco, her husband's place of work, and more details about his appearance. It turned out the only distinguishing feature he had was a scar on his neck and shoulder which was the result of him pulling a pan of boiling water over himself when he was a nipper. Not terribly helpful to me unless Walter went around shirtless. My client did, however, provide me with a photograph of her hubby – a sepia studio portrait taken just after the end of the war. Like so many men, he had been eager to dispose of the uniform he'd worn during the conflict and to don a pin-striped double-breasted affair to establish his residency in civvy street once more. The face that stared back at me was surprisingly undistinguished. I had expected a handsome fellow, matching his wife's attractiveness, but here was a bland-looking chap with a fairly comical pencil moustache which appeared as though it had been drawn on above his upper lip rather than grown there. Perhaps Walter Clements had a magnetic personality, although it certainly wasn't evident from his photograph.

Then came the pleasant part of the interview – pleasant to me at least – the matter of fees: £2 a day plus expenses, with £20 upfront. Fortunately, Mrs Clements had come prepared. She lifted a brown envelope from her bag and extracted four crisp white fivers and placed them rather like a religious offering on the desk before me. Gauging the remaining wad in the envelope, I rather wished I'd asked for a higher fee. Selling washing machines must be quite lucrative – certainly more so than playing detective, which in my experience brings one in regular contact with the breadline.

I assured my pretty client that I would get onto the case at once and that I would report to her within three days (certainly before the money ran out). She seemed reasonably pleased with this arrangement and departed, leaving behind a faint aroma of perfume and pungent femininity.

With twenty pounds in my wallet, I wasn't about to turn into a bloodhound straight away. Not now when I could afford a late breakfast fry up at Benny's café. That would certainly set me up to face the rigours of finding a washing machine salesman who had gone AWOL.

CHAPTER THREE
From the journal of Johnny Hawke

Of all the aspects of my life in the last ten years, there has been one remarkable fixed point: Benny's Café in Soho and its owner, a little Jewish squib of a fellow who has been one of the greatest boons to me. Over the years, he has melded into the role of Father, Father Confessor, Fount of All Wisdom (not always reliable) and Bane of My Life. I love the old irritating rascal to bits, although I'd never tell him so. With my quartet of crisp white notes in my wallet, I headed at a brisk pace for his place on Old Compton Street. As I approached the brightly lit steamed up windows of the café, my mouth was already watering at the thought of bacon, egg, beans and, with luck, a fat sausage doused in brown sauce with some margarine bread on the side. Food of the Gods. How he managed such luxury for one and six with rationing still in place, I had no idea and wasn't about to ask.

The place was half full, mainly men catching a bite to eat on the way to work or after finishing a night shift. They were, I guessed, mainly loyal regulars. Certainly, I had seen some of these fellows stuffing their faces in here before. Benny was scuttling between the tables, collecting plates and delivering an omelette, wearing his signature long white apron tied around his waist and a puckered frown on his face. His expression hardly changed when he saw me.

'Ah, the wanderer returns,' he said in greeting. 'I thought perhaps you had lost your memory and forgotten where we are.'

'Been a bit low on funds.'

'So what. You could always owe me. You, I trust, though I ought to have my head examined.' He popped behind the counter and dropped the dirty plates into the sink. His new assistant Gino, a middle-aged Italian, was already engrossed in washing up duties.

'And now you are flush with moolah, you intend to fill your skinny frame with the delights found in Benny's Café, eh?'

17

I grinned. 'That's about it. One of your breakfast specials, garcon, with a mug of that brown stuff you profess is tea.'

'Less of the cheek or I won't slip you a fried tomato for nothing.'

'For nothing…? You feeling OK?'

'Now stop being a naughty boy. Take a seat and I'll bring you your food shortly.'

I did as I was told. I picked up the paper that the previous customer had left behind on the table and quickly perused the pages. The news was hardly more encouraging than when Hitler was bombarding the city. I noted that soap rationing was being brought to a close so we all could get very clean again soon, but there was still all the other kinds of rationing in place like meat, tea, butter, sugar, and smiling. The paper also informed me that conscription was being extended by a further two years, clearly indicating that although the war had been over for five years, we still did not live in a safe world.

The food arrived quickly, including the promised fried tomato. I attacked it with gusto. Benny pulled up a chair and watched me in silence while I demolished his tasty fare.

'That was good,' I said, smiling as I pushed my empty plate to one side.

'Of course it was. Have you ever been disappointed with any of the food I have placed before you?'

I raised my eyebrows and pulled out a packet of cigarettes. 'Let's remain friends, eh?' I said with a smile and offered Benny a cigarette.

'How you been keeping, Johnny? You look a little pale,' he said seriously, a note of concern in his voice.

I hated it when Benny took on his mother hen mantle. He'd had no children of his own and so, to him, I was his big kid whom he loved to cosset. As an orphan, I had grown up without the love of a mother and father and so I had learned to fend for myself. I didn't need or want this kind of attention and besides, I was a big boy now. However, I knew that Benny only acted out of kindness.

'I am a little pale. Everyone in this great big city is a little pale. Fresh air and sunshine seem to be in short supply.'

'Tell me about it. Every time we get one of those thick foggy smoggy things my business goes down the pan.'

That was another of his hobby horses: moaning about how badly his takings were. It was a perennial claim that any day now he would go out of business. Both he and I knew this was rubbish. Benny had survived the horrors and devastation of the blitz and all the inconveniences of post-war Britain and he was still here serving his simple fare to the locals of Soho.

'How's young Peter?' he asked, changing tack again.

'He's doing fine. I had a letter from him last week. Everything seems to be going swimmingly.'

'He's in Edinburgh now?'

I nodded. Peter was a young runaway orphan boy I had sort of adopted unofficially, or perhaps it would be more appropriate to say that he had adopted me at the beginning of the war. With Benny's help, we had seen him through his education and his adolescence. He had always been fascinated by my work as a detective and initially had wanted to join me as a junior partner, but there really wasn't enough security or future in my line of work. I survived, but only just, and I wanted a better, more secure existence for him. Eventually, Peter enlisted in the police force, sailed through his induction course at the Hendon Police College and was now strutting the streets of Edinburgh in his sergeant's uniform. I was convinced he'd be in plain clothes within twelve months. Detective work, but with a regular salary and career prospects.

'And how's your business. Got any murders to solve?' asked Benny with gentle irony.

'Things have been slow. But I got a new client today, hence my breakfast extravagance.'

'I'm pleased for you, my boy.'

At this point, four men entered the café, chatting noisily and grabbing a table by the window. 'Now *my* business calls,' grinned Benny, rising quickly. 'Come in again soon, Johnny. It's time we had a long chin wag.'

I smiled and nodded, touching my old friend on the arm. It wasn't much of a gesture but Benny understood.

After a tortuous tube journey from central London, I eventually found myself on the dull but genteel streets of Enfield. The Klenco offices were on the outskirts of the town, so I took a taxi. It was a large building which housed offices of four companies, including the washing machine folk. I passed through the revolving doors and found myself in an echoing foyer where I consulted the list by the elevator. Klenco was on the top floor. I whizzed up there in a jiffy and came to my first hurdle: a smart bespectacled secretary-type lady sitting behind a desk who was typing at a ferocious speed. As I approached, her flying fingers stopped abruptly and she gazed up at me with an expression that appeared to be a mixture of irritation and disdain.

'Can I help you?' she said in a tone that was diametrically opposed to the sentiment of the utterance. She sounded as though she had no intention of helping me. Her fierce, unwavering stare supported that impression. I had met the type before: minions who hold the keys to the inner sanctum which gives them a certain power which they take great pleasure in wielding.

'Your managing director...' I said cheerily, with a smile.

'Yes?'

'Mr...?'

'Sanders.'

'Yes, that's him. I'd like to see him?'

My new lady friend rolled her eyes. 'Do you have an appointment?'

'No.'

Her red lips tightened into a junior snarl. 'Mr Sanders does not see anyone without an appointment'.

I withdrew my old police warrant card from my pocket and flashed it in front of her gorgon eyes. The card was at least ten years old and definitely out of date but Miss Chilly Pants was not to know that.

'He'll see me,' I said sternly. 'Police. A matter of national emergency. Life and death.'

She stared for a few moments, mesmerised by the card, her sharp features registering indecision and uncertainty. I smiled inwardly: I had hooked her.

'I need to see him... now. Understand?' I added tartly.

It gave me great pleasure to see the ice maiden, stern guardian at the gates of Klenco, completely flustered. I twisted the knife. 'You don't want to find yourself arrested for hindering a police investigation, do you?'

She shook her head. 'Just wait a minute,' she said, all the arrogance having melted away. She rose quickly from her desk and headed down the corridor. I smiled and replaced the warrant card. It had done the trick yet again.

Mr Roland Sanders – his nameplate was on his desk – was a plump, rosy-cheeked fellow with little piggy eyes and receding red hair. He was dressed in an expensive, well-cut double-breasted suit and was smoking a small cigar. There was an aura of arrogance and self-satisfaction about his demeanour that made me dislike him immediately. His ample figure prompted me to think of him as Roly Poly Sanders.

'I hope this won't take long,' he said, failing to offer me a seat.

'So do I,' I replied with a generous smile.

'What's it all about then? Spit it out. I haven't got all day.'

'It's about one of your employees...'

'Oh?'

'Walter Clements.'

'Who?'

I took the photograph of my client's husband from my pocket and placed it on the desk in front of Roly Poly. 'This fellow,' I said. 'Walter Clements. He's one of your salesmen.'

Roly Poly gazed at the photograph for a time and then threw me a basilisk stare. 'Is this some kind of joke? I've never seen this man before in my life, and I can assure you we have no one of the name Walter Clements working for Klenco.'

CHAPTER FOUR

Snowdrop.

That was the safe house. Clements knew of it. Had been told about it but had never visited the place. He had been informed that the refuge had only to be used in emergencies and, in his naivety, had foolishly assumed that he would never have the need to visit the place or to take advantage of its facilities. He wasn't ever going to be in that kind of danger. He had been wrong.

Almost like a zombie, he made his way there, his mind frozen with one thought: 'the game's up'. Only it wasn't a game, was it, Wally? As he ran this phrase through his mind, he began to shake with fear. What was to happen to him now? He dreaded to think and so he didn't. He had visited Kings Cross and retrieved the package of money that he kept in a box there. He knew that he couldn't put what he had considered lightly as his 'ill-gotten gains' in the bank – so much cash would raise suspicions. And he wasn't about to bring the money home; so he stowed it here. It was, he supposed, his emergency fund if something dreadful happened. And now something dreadful had happened.

How had the beans been spilt? How on earth had they got on to him? He had been so careful. He must have slipped up in some way but for the life of him, he couldn't reason how. Perhaps it was something to do with that cleaner, the one who almost caught him with his hands in the till? But what could she know? He grunted with anger and frustration. What the hell did it matter how he had been sussed out – he had. And now he had to deal with the consequences – whatever form they may take.

Each face he passed in the crowd and on the underground seemed to be staring at him, their eyes fierce with accusations and their lips appearing to whisper the word 'traitor.' On leaving the station, he pulled his hat low over his face and hailed a taxi. Sitting in the shadowy gloom at the back of the cab gave him some sort of comfort, although the driver was intent on chatting to him, something about a recent boxing match. He muttered inarticulate replies when absolutely necessary.

He got the cab to drop him several streets away from the safe house and made the rest of the way on foot. He arrived in the late afternoon. His lips twisted into a bitter sardonic smile as he thought about the term 'safe house'. No bloody house was safe in his line of work, and particularly not now. The blow had come out of the blue. He'd had no suspicion, no hint that he'd been under surveillance.

What the hell was going to happen now? Surely they had to get him out of the country. Out of the way. God, he didn't like the possible implications of that particular phrase. He was well aware that he now presented a problem to his masters but at the same time, he had to rely on them for help. He had helped them all right, now they had to do the decent thing in return. To try and go it alone would be disastrous; then he would have two sets of hounds on his track: the Russians and the British authorities. He would be caught like the filling in a very dangerous sandwich.

He made his way up the path and round to the rear of the building – an innocent-looking detached suburban house with net curtains and a neat garden. All very bland and all very British. At the rear of the property was a set of steps down to a cellar door. Loosening the brick adjacent to the doorknob, as he had been instructed in one of his many briefings, he retrieved a key hidden in the plasterwork and unlocked the door. Stepping inside, his nostrils were assailed with the smell of damp and decay.

As he closed the door behind him, he heard a movement in the shadows and then felt the muzzle of a pistol pressing firmly on the side of his head.

'Snowdrop,' he managed to say.

There was no response. *My God*, he thought. *Is this it? Is the bastard with the gun going to pull the trigger?*

'Is that you, Chapman? Can't you bloody well see who it is?' he said, his voice a fierce rasp.

'No, not in this light,' came the reply from the shadows. 'But I recognise your voice.' The pistol was retracted. 'So, you managed to give the buggers the slip,' said Chapman lightly, as though the whole thing was some kind of joke.

'For the time being. You know all about it?'

'Almost immediately. Number One contacted me two hours ago.'

'How the hell did they find out?'

Chapman shrugged. 'No idea, old chap. They've got eyes and ears everywhere. Still, no doubt things will be sorted'. He emerged from the gloom, his broad greasy face bearing an unpleasant grin. To Clements, he looked like an overgrown schoolboy with his shiny blazer a size too small for him, his thinning hair in a permanently dishevelled state and frayed collar with a college tie hanging loosely below it.

'Come upstairs and have a drink. I am sure you could do with one. I have some rather delightful vodka which will put you in a better frame of mind,' he said, shepherding Clements to the stairs.

Bloody Chapman. The oaf thought that alcohol was the panacea for all ills. It certainly wouldn't solve his current predicament.

'What did Number One say?' Clements asked later when they were ensconced in the sitting room, each nursing a glass of neat vodka.

'Nothing much. You know him, but he told me that he will come to see you this evening to… make arrangements,' replied Chapman casually.

'What do you think is likely to happen?'

Chapman gave him an irritating smirk and shrugged his shoulders.

That unrestrained eloquent gesture seemed to tell him all. The alcohol had relaxed Clements' mind somewhat and he was now able to view the situation with greater clarity. And it was bad. The veil had lifted and he could see things as they really were with unnerving clearness. He now saw that he was eminently expendable. What use was he to them now that he had been exposed? They wouldn't take the trouble to ship him out of the country, off to Russia. What bloody use could he be to them there? His spying days were over. He was now simply surplus to requirements. He had only been a little convenient cog in their machine – and now he was an indispensable cog. It suddenly became clear to him: a swift execution was his fate. He would be dealt with quickly and discreetly, and end up in a body bag dumped somewhere. That would simplify matters for them very conveniently. As this thought settled firmly in his mind, he felt his stomach constrict and his gorge rise, the vodka inflaming his stomach. He gazed around the room and across at his companion, who was still nursing the pistol in his lap. A sense of panic took hold of him. He had to escape. It has been a mistake to come here. He was like a mouse who had happily trodden on the trap thinking it was safe. He could not stay here waiting for the inevitable. Clements knew he had to flee this place.

'You still have the microfilm?' It was a casual query from Chapman but he knew it was a key question. No doubt the greasy-faced fellow had been instructed by Number One to find out. That little treasure had to be retrieved first before anything could be done with him.

'Yes, I still have the film.'

'You'd better give it to me,' said Chapman, a hint of ice in his tone now and he tightened his grasp on the revolver.

Clements shook his head. 'No, I will only pass it over to Number One.'

'I think you would be wise to hand it over,' said Chapman, raising the gun and aiming it at him.

Clements shook his head. 'Can't do that even if I wanted to. I don't have it with me. Don't worry. It's in a safe place. I'll make sure it lands safely in Number One's hands. Now how about another drink?'

Chapman scowled. It was clear he wasn't sure whether he could believe Clements or not. 'Help yourself,' he snapped.

Clements nodded dumbly and moved towards the table where the bottle stood. 'A large one, I think,' he said casually.

He picked up the bottle, poured himself a generous measure and, still clasping the bottle, began to wander back to his seat. His route took him behind Chapman's chair. With a swift and violent motion, he brought the bottle down hard on the man's skull. Chapman uttered a muffled groan and he slumped forward, gradually sliding to the floor.

Clements stepped around the body and repeated the blow, just to be sure the man was well and truly unconscious. Then, snatching up the gun and slipping it into his coat pocket, he made his way to the door. *Now*, he thought, *I am really on my own. I have become the filling in that dangerous sandwich. Now I have to disappear.*

As he made his down the street away from the safe house, a thought struck him. Frances! He knew that he would probably never see her again… but he must warn her not to go to the police about him – about his absence. The longer they were kept out of the matter the better. In his mind, he concocted a note to send her that should delay her from taking any action for a while. That should buy him a little extra time… he hoped.

CHAPTER FIVE

Some days later in a well-appointed townhouse in London, the red telephone rang. It was an elegant, discreet ring. Sir Jeremy reached out, lifted the receiver and listened.

The caller identified himself.

'Go ahead,' said Sir Jeremy.

'I'm afraid there is still no news about Clements.'

Sir Jeremy gave a grunt of irritation. 'Has he become the invisible man? For God's sake, he's not a trained agent. A bloody amateur. A jumped-up clerk. How on earth can he be giving us the runaround?'

'He's gone to earth somewhere…'

'I am well aware of that. It's your bloody job to find out where that somewhere is!'

There was an awkward pause down the line and then the voice started up again.

'I'm afraid there's more, sir. Apparently, the wife has been in touch with a private detective. A John Hawke. He has an office at Christopher Court off Tottenham Court Road. He's already been sniffing around.'

'Has he? Well, we'd better clear up this mess as quickly as possible or it could have serious damaging repercussions. It's unlikely that Clements will attempt to return home – he'll know we'll have the house under surveillance - but the woman will have to be dealt with. Get Olga and Basil on to that. As for Mr Hawke, leave him to me.'

'Very well, sir.' There was a gentle click and the line went dead.

Sir Jeremy rose from his chair, moved to the drinks cabinet and poured himself an amontillado. He returned to his desk and sipped the sherry slowly, his eyes narrowed in thought. *This Hawke, a private detective, eh? He might be of use*, he thought. *It's possible that in the end, he could unknowingly help us to track Clements down. Well, maybe.* Sir Jeremy pondered further, then reached out for the telephone and dialled. The call was answered almost immediately.

'Ah, Bertie, my fount of all wisdom. A few words to the wise. A private detective called John Hawke. What can you tell me about him?'

There was a throaty chuckle at the other end of the line and then a rough Cockney voice rambled on for some five minutes. Sir Jeremy made notes as he listened intently.

'Thank you, Bertie, I knew I could rely on you and that encyclopaedic brain of yours. You've never let me down yet.'

Another throaty chuckle and then the line went dead.

Sir Jeremy afforded himself a gentle smile as he dialled once more.

'Hello, it's me,' he said softly when the call was answered. 'How are you?'

He nodded with pleasure at the reply. 'Well, you'll be pleased to know I have a job for you.'

CHAPTER SIX
From the journal of Johnny Hawke

I left the offices of Klenco with my tail between my legs. I'd hit a few brick walls in my time, but not one as well constructed and sturdy as this brute. On my return to the city from Enfield on the overcrowded tube, my mind was in free fall. What the hell was going on here? Apparently, a husband disappears but warns his wife not to contact the police – this is a husband who has been lying to the lady about the nature of his employment. Walter C isn't a washing machine salesman and he doesn't work for Klenco. However, I only had Mrs Frances Clements' word for the whole twisted scenario. Who was lying to who? One thing was for sure: I was being led up the garden path. And that made me angry.

It was dusk when I emerged from the underground station and suddenly I felt weary and in need of a drink. I certainly wasn't in the mood to tackle my client with the news – if it was news – that her husband had other fish to fry instead of selling washing machines – if you'll pardon my mixed metaphor. I wandered into The Jack Horner for a pint of bitter. Well, at least I could afford one thanks to the largess of Madame Clements. This idea gave me pause for thought. Surely she wouldn't have passed over twenty pounds to me just to go on a wild goose chase. That would be crazy. I sat at a corner table sipping my pint and thinking hard, trying to work out what on earth was going on. I reckoned that the sooner I found out, the sooner my brain would stop aching. I couldn't wait until tomorrow to sort things out. I had to make a start tonight. Strike while the iron etc. Decision made, I drank up my pint quickly and headed back to the tube station. I just had to visit my lady client this evening to see if I could clear up this little mystery. If I didn't, then I knew this rather dark conundrum would keep me awake all night. I checked in my notebook. She lived in King Henry's Walk, Islington.

After enduring two tortuous stuffy tube journeys in one day, I decided to splash out on the luxury of a cab to take me to the address. 4 King Henry's Walk was a smart brick villa on a quiet street. It was quite dark now as I approached the front door but I could see chinks of light escaping down the side of the sitting room curtains. I was in luck, the lady was at home. Perhaps hubby was also in residence, having returned with another cock and bull story involving washing machines and difficult customers.

I knocked heartily and waited. It wasn't long before I heard some activity in the hallway, followed by the turning of the key. The door opened and a woman peered out at me. She was backlit by the light in the hall but I could see that it wasn't Frances Clements.

Here was a stout creature in her forties, possibly on the brink of fifty. She was heavily made up in a tartish way and wore a tight pencil skirt and a low cut frilly blouse.

'Yes, what do you want?' she asked brusquely in a voice that had a trace of an accent. I couldn't put my finger on it but I could tell that she wasn't a native of this island.

'I'm looking for Mrs Frances Clements,' I said, doffing my hat.

'Who?'

I repeated the name.

She shook her head. 'Never heard of her. She does not live here.'

I opened my mouth to speak but then I realised I really didn't know what to say. My new acquaintance had covered the ground in two short sentences: she had never heard of Frances Clements and she asserted that didn't live there. What more could I ask? Any questions would simply prompt a string of negative responses.

I raised my hat again, gave a gentlemanly nod and said: 'Sorry to have bothered you.'

She pursed her lips and mouthed some expletive under her breath before slamming the door in my face.

With leaden feet, I made my way back to the tube station. What, I pondered glumly, was going on? This was like some surrealistic dream. People were disappearing and I had no idea as to the reason. I could concoct theories as to why Mr Clements would lie about his job and fly the marital coup, but not why my client, who had handed over a very tidy sum of cash to retain my services, should also lie. What was the purpose? I was nowhere near Billingsgate market but I could smell something very fishy in the air. The problem was, I had no idea what.

It was too late to do anything about it now. I would just wander home, indulge in a whisky nightcap and sleep on it. Possibly in the morning, with a bit of luck, I would discover that this whole day had been an unpleasant dream.

Dawn did not so much break as squeeze itself into the leaden sky and on waking I found that the previous day had not been a dream after all. I noted that I still had most of my mysterious client's retaining fee and a confusing scenario to deal with. In a mechanical fashion, I attended to my ablutions with more speed than usual while I played around in my mind with the problem of the disappearing Clements. I could, I suppose, forget about the whole thing. If some tricksy lady was happy to pay me twenty quid to go off on a pointless wild goose chase, so be it. Her loss, my gain. However, at the same time, I had been engaged in my professional capacity as a private detective to find her husband. Wasn't it my duty to try a little harder? And then there was my innate curiosity. I was both intrigued and frustrated by the way events had fallen out yesterday. I really wanted to get to the bottom of this mystery. All well and good. But how?

Perhaps another of Benny's breakfasts would kick start the brain cells into creative action and provide me with a plan of action. If that failed, at least I would have a full belly.

It was just after nine when I took my seat in Benny's Café and ordered the usual fry up.

'Two days in a row,' crooned mine host. 'Business must be good.'

'You don't know the half of it.'

'Really? You want to share half of it.'

I hesitated for a fraction of a second and then shook my head. 'Nah, just boring stuff. What I need now is not an ear to bend but a plate of grub to demolish.'

Benny gave me one of his knowing looks. 'OK,' he said and whisked himself away to the kitchen. I scanned the room as usual, looking for a discarded newspaper so I could depress myself even further with catching up on the latest news, but it seemed that on this occasion I was out of luck.

Sometime later, Benny arrived with my breakfast and I asked him if he had a paper to peruse while I scoffed. 'Have you tried buying your own, Johnny. An *Express* will only cost you two pence.'

'You know me, Benny. I'm always on an economy drive.'

He gave me a half-smile. 'I'll lend you my copy but I've a good mind to add it to the bill.'

I grinned and gave him the thumbs up. Seconds later, he slapped that day's edition of the *Daily Express* down on the table. 'And don't get any of that brown sauce on it,' he growled. He loved playing grumpy with me, but the act didn't quite work because he couldn't disguise the friendly twinkle in his eyes.

As I ate my eggs and bacon, I felt myself becoming a fully functioning human once again. Time to peruse the paper. It was the usual parade of bad news. Train fares were going up, a mine shaft had caved in at a Welsh pit with 128 miners killed, and the conflict in Korea was escalating. The correspondent reckoned that it would not be long before commonwealth forces were involved. We all thought we had done with the war in 1945 but I reckon it's like the poor, conflict will always be with us. I cast the paper aside in dismay, making my usual vow not to read one again. Those pages of tiny cramped print only brought gloom and despair. I finished my breakfast and lit a cigarette, trying to focus on my own little problem: the mysterious affair of the missing client. As I stared ahead of me, futile thoughts fluttering through my mind, I found my eyes wandering back to that blasted newspaper, and suddenly my eyes lit upon the Stop Press column. It was the headline that caught my full attention. Well, as a detective it would: BODY FOUND IN THAMES. I pulled the paper back towards me and read the brief article:

'Late last night the body of a young woman was fished out of the Thames by the River Police. She was naked and her throat had been cut. The only clues to her identity is a large mole or beauty spot on her right cheek and the diamond ring she was wearing, which was in the shape of a snake. The police are making enquiries.'

My breakfast did some kind of military manoeuvre in my stomach. Could it be? The mole, the ring. It had to be. This was too much of a coincidence. Surely this was my client, Mrs Frances Clements. I pictured those delicate fingers and that ever so chic ring circling one of them. I read the piece again slowly just to make sure. Now my mind raced and decisions were quickly made.

With some alacrity, I left my seat and headed for the counter.

'Leaving already?' said Benny. 'You should let your food settle.'

'Can I use your phone, please?' I said, cutting to the quick.

'What? First a free paper, now a free phone call.' Benny raised his arm. 'You want a blood transfusion also.'

'I'll pay for the call.'

'I should be so petty as to charge you. You know where it is. As long as you're not calling Timbuktoo.'

I grinned. 'A local call, I assure you.'

Benny nodded his head benignly.

I headed for the little cramped sitting room at the back of the café where the telephone was situated. I snatched up the receiver and dialled for the operator.

'Which number,' she enquired.

'Get me Scotland Yard.'

CHAPTER SEVEN
From the journal of Johnny Hawke

I had known David Llewellyn – now Superintendent Llewellyn – since the late 1930s when I was on the force. He had taken a liking to me as I to him and, as a senior officer – he was an Inspector then – he assumed the role of my mentor. We got on famously. I was, and indeed am, still not sure what he saw in me, but I liked his honesty, his determination to do the job well and his quirky Welsh humour. I also envied the lucky bastard for he had something which I have never succeeded in possessing: a happy home life and a sweet, beautiful wife.

We still kept in touch after I set up as a private detective. Indeed, I saw him as my contact with the official police and he sometimes came to me for off the record information or news of nefarious activities. We had shared some interesting cases over the years and had been in a few rather dangerous scrapes together. I must admit that since the war, I had not seen as much of him as hitherto; this was partly due to the less interesting nature of my investigations which did not require the police assistance David could provide and the fact that he had climbed up the slippery career pole to his now exalted rank.

After a fair time of waiting on the phone and being passed to one department to another, I eventually managed to reach David's office at the Yard. At length, I heard his rich baritone. 'Is that really my old mucker Hawke on the line or is this a hoax call,' he said cheerfully.

'No it really is I, Jonathan Hawke, desperate detective and spinster of the parish.'

He guffawed. 'What can I do for you, lad?'

It was a long time since anyone had addressed me as 'lad' and it made me smile. 'Are you involved in this affair of the woman fished out of the Thames last night? Throat cut,' I asked.

'I know of the matter, but I'm not handling the case personally. Why?'

'I think I might know who she is.'

34

'Really, boyo. At the moment I won't ask why, but if you can provide a name for the poor creature, that will be a bonus.'

'I'll have to see her to be sure.'

'Of course. Just a mo.' David placed the receiver down and I could hear vague mumblings in the background. After a couple of minutes, he came back on the line. 'At the moment the lass is in the Viney Street morgue.'

'I know it.'

'Good. I'll meet you there in about an hour. Say eleven o'clock. Can you make it?'

'Yes, I can. See you there.'

'I'll wear a carnation in my lapel so you'll recognise me.'

I could hear him still chuckling at his own joke as he put down the phone.

Morgues. Despite the fact that I've been in a fair number of them in my time, entering these houses of the dead does not get any easier for me. The sight of a naked corpse, usually one whose body has received some obscene wound, is perhaps the grimmest experience I know. In the presence of a mutilated dead person, I fear for the reliability of my bowels. I know many coppers take such experiences in their stride, viewing these victims as just pieces of dead meat which may or may not provide some evidence to help them with their enquiries, squashing their human empathy in pursuit of a case. Not me. I am more than conscious that the lifeless inhabitants of these grim places were but a few hours previously living, breathing people with aspirations and hopes for the future. They did not expect to lie naked on a cold slab as a police exhibit with an identification tag attached to their big toe.

David was waiting for me as I turned up at the entrance of the police morgue on Viney Street, just a truncheon's throw from Scotland Yard. It was good to see him again. He looked very much the same as he has done for years. His square-jawed features were topped by a mop of blonde hair which looked as though it had never seen a comb. He was tall with broad shoulders and an athletic body, which always seemed to be on the verge of bursting out of his clothes, but the eyes revealed a sharpness of mind and keen intelligence. We shook hands, patted each other on the back and exchanged a few pleasantries before we entered the morgue. David had phoned ahead and so we were swiftly escorted into the chamber which was coyly labelled 'The Waiting Room'. There on a trolley covered by a long white sheet – a kind of shroud I suppose – was the body we had come to see.

With practised skill, like a magician's assistant, the attendant pulled back the sheet to reveal the whole body of the unfortunate underneath. I moved closer and examined the face, feeling the gorge rise in my throat. It was a ghastly sight. The skin was the colour of putty and had a damp sheen to it, as though the body had been sculpted out of some unpleasant malleable material. The head had almost been severed from the rest of the body, the terrible blood-tinged wound at the neck resembling a horrific second mouth. I gazed at the twisted features and the eyes which were held wide with fear at the moment of death. There was no doubt about it: this was the woman who had sat in my office the previous day, the woman who had handed me twenty pounds and asked me to find her husband, the woman who was Mrs Frances Clements.

I turned to David and nodded.

'You sure?'

I nodded again. 'What about the ring?' I asked.

The attendant stepped forward and handed me a small cardboard box. I opened it. Inside, nestling on a small sheet of crumpled tissue paper was the gold snake ring with the large diamond still sparkling with life – unlike its owner.

'This clinches it. This is the ring.'

David clapped me on the shoulder. 'Good man. Now I think you could do with a drink. You've gone green at the gills since we came in here.'

'A drink would be good.' I handed the box back to the attendant with what I hoped was a smile of thanks but I feared looked like a twisted grimace.

Once outside the morgue and I was able to breathe in the fresh air again, I began to come round from that unpleasant experience. 'You did say whisky?' I said.

David rolled his eyes. 'I said drink. Although I was thinking of a pot of tea.'

'If you were, it would be for the first time.'

David laughed. 'The Red Lion is only a few streets away. We can have a natter there.'

'And a whisky.'

'Yes, all right, and a whisky.'

Ten minutes later we were ensconced in a quiet corner of The Red Lion. In fact, every corner was quiet at the moment, the pub having only just opened. I had a double scotch in front of me and David was taking the first sip of his pint of bitter. The whisky was already working its magic, warming up my frozen bones and reviving my spirits.

David gave a satisfied sigh and leaned back in his chair. 'So, boyo, let's have the low down. You say this dead lady was a client. Fill in the details.'

I did so. I told David how Mrs Frances Clements came to me because her husband had gone missing and when I visited his supposed place of work in Enfield, the managing director had no knowledge of the man. When I went to inform Mrs Clements of this fact at the address she'd given me, it was a case of déjà vu. She wasn't known at that address either.

David gave a dark chuckle. 'A mystery at both ends of the case, eh? You do pick 'em, Johnny.'

I shook my head. '*They* pick me,' I said sadly.

'I suppose you have no idea who wanted to do the lady in and chuck her in the river.'

'Well, the obvious choice is her husband, I suppose, but I have no notion why he should want to do that – or, to be frank, if he is alive.'

'There's a thought. Well, I reckon the next move is to try and find this phantom hubby, Walter Clements – if that is his real name. Do you have a description of him?'

'I've something better than that. I have a photograph.' I retrieved it from my inner pocket. 'It's about four years old, I guess.'

David examined the photograph. 'Fairly nondescript chappie.

No really strong distinguishing features. I'll take this and run it through police records and see if he's been a naughty boy in the past.'

I was reluctant to let the photograph go, but I realised that David's notion was a good one.

'I'll let you know if we turn up anything. I'll let you have the photo back in due course. In the meantime, what are you going to do?'

I shrugged my shoulders. 'Finish this scotch and meander back to my office and think.'

It was a lie. That was not what I intended to do, but I had to give myself some leeway in this matter – it was my case after all. My client was dead. I had to be true to my code and find her killer. I said cheerio to David on the pavement outside the Red Lion, agreeing to keep in touch, and made my way to the tube while he returned to the Yard. I travelled once more to Islington. One little thought was niggling away at the back of my mind. It was growing in size and importance. It had struck me that I had perhaps been a little gullible in accepting the word of that stout lady who answered the door to 4 King Henry's Walk, asserting that she had never heard of Frances Clements and that she certainly didn't live there. There was rather a lot of subterfuge in this affair and this could be yet another example. I had been a little dim to take a word on trust. It was time to rectify that.

I made my way down the neat little street to number 4 and surveyed the property from the pavement. There was no sign of life. All the curtains were closed, which was a little odd for the afternoon. I decided to try my luck again and knocked heartily on the door. As I expected there was no reply. I was about to try again when I sensed a presence behind me. I turned swiftly to face a tall, skeletal postman with an envelope in his hand.

'Afternoon, squire,' he greeted me cheerily. 'Would you mind popping this through the letterbox for me?' He proffered the envelope.

'Sure,' I said with a smile and did as he asked but not before casting a close glance at the envelope. I could see that it was addressed to a 'Mrs Frances Clements.' Bingo! So she did live here – or to be more accurate, she had lived here.

'Thanks,' chirped the postie as he made his way down the street.

I waited a while until he disappeared from sight and the checking there was no one else about and that the coast, as they say in detective novels, was clear. I whipped out my clever bit of wire for dealing with locks. I reckoned if the house was empty, as I thought, I would have no trouble in gaining entry without disturbing anyone. However, if the door was bolted on the inside and there was someone lurking within, that would need a very different procedure.

As luck would have it, after about a minute of practised twisting and turning, I heard the satisfying click as the lock mechanism released itself. Within a trice, I was inside.

I stood for a moment in the gloomy hallway and listened. There was not a sound. It was as though I were in a ghost house. Moving down the hall, I passed through a door on the left into the kitchen. There was evidence of recent activity in here. There were dirty dishes in the sink – two plates, two cups and saucers with supporting cutlery which told me that two people had been dining here and I reckoned neither of them was Mrs Frances Clements. It must be Stout Lady and partner – or should I say, accomplice.

Further scrutiny revealed nothing of significance apart from an ashtray with several stubs of the Player's variety.

I moved across the hall into the sitting room. It was very well appointed: thick carpet, fine three-piece suite, cocktail cabinet and a large radiogram. Just the sort of pad I expected the late Mrs Clements to have. The cushions on the sofa were dented so someone had been sitting there quite recently. What on earth had gone on here? Had Stout Lady and pal invaded the premises and killed Mrs C? That was the reasonable scenario presented to me at the moment. But why should they wish to do away with an apparently innocent woman and who the hell were they? The imponderables were building up by the minute. With this thought, I made my way upstairs. Here there were two bedrooms and a bathroom. The smaller of the two bedrooms was pristine. It didn't look as though it had been used for some time. The linen on the bed was smooth and uncreased. However, the larger bedroom told a different tale. It had all the ambience of a film star's boudoir, ruched drapes, gold lamp shades and silk sheets on the bed – but these, unlike those in the small bedroom, were tangled in great disarray, as though someone had spent a very disturbed night. However, when I pulled back the top sheet, what I saw made my heart skip a beat. There was a large red crusty stain, roughly the shape of Australia. Dried blood – quite a quantity of it. So, I reasoned, the poor woman had been killed here before being taken away and dumped in the river. I grimaced at the thought and then I grimaced even more when it struck me that when I had called here last evening and was told the pack of lies by Stout Lady, poor Frances Clements may well have been alive. Had I been a little less gullible and had more savvy I might have… But, hey, Johnny, I told myself, don't go wandering down those crazy cul de sacs. You can't change the past, only influence the future.

After this mental slap on the wrists, I forced myself to focus on the matter in hand and carried out a thorough search of the room. Dropping to my knees and peering under the bed, I saw a knife. It glinted obscenely in the dusty gloom. A large savage kitchen thing with a serrated edge, tinged with dark dried blood. This no doubt was the murder weapon. Tearing a strip off one of the unsullied sheets, I pushed the bed aside enough allow me to slip the material over the weapon and retrieve it without contaminating it with my fingerprints. This may be of use to David and the boffins at the Yard, although it was most likely the killer had wiped his or her dabs off the handle before disposing of it under the bed.

I slipped the knife into the inside pocket of my overcoat. Obviously, Stout Woman was involved in the murder, but she must have had at least one more accomplice in order to restrain Frances Clements and slit her throat. The teacups downstairs bore witness to that. And surely Number Two had to be a man… That much seemed clear, but the rest of the matter had the clarity of a thick mulligatawny soup.

As I pondered this, there came a loud knocking at the front door. I felt my frame stiffen in apprehension. What now? Who was a calling? It was unlikely to be the villains returning to the scene of their crime. Why should they, and they certainly wouldn't knock. It could be any kind of tradesman or maybe a friend. If the latter, they might be able to furnish me with more information about Mrs Clements and her hubby.

As I returned to the ground floor, the knocking recommenced. I opened the door, and standing before me was a pretty young woman in a dark coat with a fir trim. She was carrying a large suitcase. Her eyes widened in surprise when she saw me and for a moment seemed lost for words, but at length, she spoke: 'Who are you?'

The hard ones first.

'I'm John, a friend of the family.'

The frown on the young woman's face informed me that she was not convinced by my assertion.

'Where is my sister?' she said.

'Your sister?' My voice went up a register.

'Yes, my sister, Frances.'

'I think you'd better come in.'

'I think I had.'

We moved from the hall into the sitting room.

'Where is she then and what are you doing in her house?'

'I'm afraid she is not here.'

'What do you mean? She called me yesterday and asked me to come today. You say you're a friend of the family. I've never seen you before or heard Frances mention any friend of hers called John.'

There was no way around this situation. Dislike it as I did, I knew that I had to shoot from the hip.

'I am a private detective. Your sister hired me...'

Her eyes widened. 'Ah, you must be the man called Hawke.'

'Yes. John Hawke. You know about me?'

'Only that Frances hired a man called Hawke to find out where her husband, Walter, had gone. He'd not been home for a few days. She asked me to come and stay with her until the matter was resolved. Has it been resolved?'

I shook my head. 'Far from it, I'm afraid.'

'Where is Frances now?' She was growing angry and frustrated and I knew that I couldn't prevaricate any longer.

I took a deep breath and ran with it. 'I'm sorry to say that your sister...' I faltered, not wanting to deliver the blow.

'What? Something is very wrong here'. Her eyes clouded with apprehension.

'Yes. I'm afraid Frances is dead...'

I didn't get a chance to say any more because the girl threw herself at me, arms flailing.

'You bastard. You liar,' she cried, her fists beating my chest. As gently as I could, I grabbed both arms and held them still. Angry tears dribbled down her face.

'I wouldn't lie to you,' I said softly. 'It is true, I'm afraid, but I had nothing to do with it. Believe me. Her death came as much as a surprise to me...' I gave up on that clumsy sentiment halfway through.

She pulled away from me, her shoulders bowed, her features drained. 'I don't understand. Is it true? Is it really true?'

'Yes,' I said. 'I am afraid so.'

Her body shuddered with emotion. 'Dead. No.' She shook her head furiously as though that would eliminate the thought, the reality.

I just nodded dumbly to reaffirm my statement.

The girl slumped down in a chair, placing her head in her hands.

'You need a drink,' I said, hurrying to the cocktail cabinet and pouring out a generous measure of brandy. 'Here you are. Take a good slurp,' I said, proffering the glass.

Slowly, she raised her head and gazed at me in bewilderment. 'Fran is dead? Really?'

I gave her another solemn nod.

'Oh, my God.'

I pushed the glass closer and she took it with both hands and drank.

'How... how did it happen?'

It was no time for prevarication. 'She was murdered,' I said softly. 'Someone came to the house and...'

'Murdered! My God! This is a nightmare. Surely I'm going to wake up anytime now.'

I said nothing but my expression must have told her that this was no dream.

'And what have you to do with all this…?' she asked.

'My name is Hawke. John Hawke. I am a private detective…'

'Yes, yes, I know that. You're the man Fran employed to try and find Walter. Have you found him?'

I shook my head. 'No, I am afraid not. And when I came here to report back to your sister last night a woman answered the door and said that she'd never heard of her.'

'Who was this woman?'

'I don't know, but it is most likely that she is implicated in the murder in some way.'

'Murder… that word again. She really is dead…?'

'I am so sorry.'

'What happened?'

I gave her a basic outline of the matter, trying hard not to dwell on the gruesome details.

'Oh, this is oh so terrible. Who would want to … to kill Fran?'

'That's what I intend to find out.'

'Where is my sister now?'

'She is … with the police authorities.'

'I want to see her.'

'I am sure that can be arranged, but perhaps it's best to wait until tomorrow to allow yourself a little time to get your head around what's happened.'

She drained the glass of brandy and slumped back in the chair. 'Oh, my God, what a mess. Poor Fran'. Once again she put her head in her hands and sobbed, her shoulders heaving with emotion. I stood by her side and let her get on with it. Nothing I could say or do would ease matters at this present moment. It was best to let her cry it out. No doubt there would be other similar sessions in the next few days. It's human nature when you lose someone close to you. I know only too well.

Eventually, she attempted to pull herself together. Now I could do something positive. I offered her my handkerchief. 'I don't know your name.'

'It's Susan. Susan Kershaw,' she sniffled, drying her eyes.

'Well, I think the best thing, for now, is to get you home and I'll sort things out with the authorities for you to see your sister, maybe tomorrow. No doubt the police will want to interview you.'

She shook her head. 'I can't go home now. I live in Brighton. I came up to town to be with Fran while things… I just need to stay in London until this whole terrible mess is cleared up.'

'Well,' I said, 'you can't stay here, that's for sure.' I did not add that this house was now a murder scene and the property would be placed off-limits to all by the police investigation team.

'I'll have to book myself into a hotel. Could you help me find one?'

'Of course. Shall we go? There's nothing either of us can do here now.'

She shivered. 'Yes. I'd really like to leave.'

I helped to her feet and she smiled sadly. 'I'm sorry I went for you. I don't know what I was thinking. It's just a terrible dream'

'I know,' I said softly. 'You were shocked and upset. It's fine.'

We left the house and I tried to reverse the unlocking procedure with my little implement, but I was not as adept at this and I was struggling when Susan said, 'You don't have to do that. I've got a key.'

I grinned and this prompted another shy smile from her.

As we moved down the path, I noticed a car, a grey Daimler saloon, parked a few yards down the road. I could see the silhouettes of the two occupants. Suddenly, the engine revved up and the vehicle began to move forward. As it did so, the passenger window was wound down. Having been in the detective business for around ten years and having found myself in some seriously sticky scrapes, I have developed a kind of sixth sense when danger is about to rear its head. That sixth sense began to wave its flag in a very vigorous fashion. I paused on the path, wrapping my arm around the girl just as I saw an arm extend from the open window of the car.

The hand held a gun.

CHAPTER EIGHT
From the journal of Johnny Hawke

It did not need an Einstein to realise what was happening. In an instant, I dragged Susan down onto the lawn just as the shot rang out. I heard the bullet whistle above our heads, and then came another shot before the car roared off down the road. I lay still for a while, the girl shuddering and whimpering with terror by my side. Then, crouching low, I made my way to the gateway and peered into the street. The car had disappeared and there was no one about. The danger, I reckoned, was over – for now.

I returned to Susan and helped her to her feet. She was in some state of shock and gazed at me with wide terrified eyes.

'We're OK. Whoever it was has gone,' I said gently. 'Let's get a taxi and high tail it out of here.'

'What's going on? What on earth…?' Words failed her.

They failed me also. Too many weird and disparate things were happening all at once and nothing made complete sense. I had wandered into a violent and mystifying maze and I had no idea which way to turn or where the next danger lay. And the poor girl must have wondered why her normal world had transformed itself into a violent nightmare. She stared at me with haunted eyes.

'I don't know what's happening,' I replied truthfully, adding, 'but I intend to find out. That's something to think about later. Come on, let's go.'

I guided her down the path and into the street, heading for the main thoroughfare, in search of a taxi.

This harmless little case of a missing husband was spinning out of control. Not only was there murder involved, but after the recent incident, it was clear that my personal safety, and possibly that of the dead woman's sister, was at risk. Was it me or Susan who had been the target of those shots? Surely it had to be me, Mr Busybody Hawke, sticking his nose into matters that did not concern him. On reflection, to my mind, it all hinged on Walter Clements. He was the real mystery factor in this affair. Whether he was a villain or a pawn, he had to be found.

Once we were ensconced in the dark confines of a taxi, Susan stopped shivering and began to calm down a little.

'They were trying to kill us, weren't they?' she asked.

'Kill me, I think.'

'Why?'

I shrugged my shoulders. 'I don't know.' The words came slowly. I hated to admit it verbally. It did not do my self-esteem as a private detective much good. All I had seemed to say to her since we met was 'I don't know.' What kind of dumb detective must she think I was? 'But I'll work it out, don't you worry,' I added in a desperate attempt to give myself some credibility.

I took Susan back to my place. I knew she couldn't stay in a hotel now, not with gun-toting villains on the prowl. However, I reckoned I knew where I could billet her – but first I needed to get her warm, relaxed and find out a little more about her sister and the phantom Walter.

Half an hour later, Susan was sitting on my lumpy couch before a noisily popping gas fire, cradling a mug of strong, hot tea and munching a garibaldi biscuit, while I popped into my office to make a couple of phone calls. I had phoned David at the Yard, giving him details of the developing saga, including the fact that he had a crime scene on his hand and that I had confiscated the murder weapon. He said he'd arrange for a constable from the local cop shop to call round for it at my place. As for Susan, I told him what I had in mind and he agreed, saying he'd like to interview her as soon as she was settled, but there was no urgent rush. 'I'm sure you'll pass on anything relevant she tells you, won't you, boyo?' I told him I would… with crossed fingers.

I then made another call before returning to my living room.

I sat opposite Susan as she drank her tea. She gazed up at me and gave me a brief sardonic smile. 'This all seems like a bad dream. I just want to wake up.' she said, shaking her head. 'It's unreal. There are so many questions… Fran, why would anyone want to kill her?'

'Possibly because she became too inquisitive.'

'What do you mean?'

'No doubt she told you that Walter left a note saying that she was not to go to the police.'

She nodded.

'Well, she didn't go to the police, but she did come to me, a fellow who could easily sniff out the truth behind Walter's disappearance. There is somebody, possibly old Walter himself, who doesn't want anyone to find out where he is and they are prepared to kill to discover his whereabouts.'

Susan gave an involuntary shudder.

'Tell me about Walter. What do you know of him?'

'Now that you ask, I realise I actually know very little about him to be honest. I only met him a couple of times. I never quite liked him. I don't know why. He was perfectly pleasant with me and he seemed to take good care of Fran but…'

'But…?'

'He somehow never seemed genuine – as though he was acting a part. Reading lines rather than being himself.'

'How long had he and Fran been married?'

Susan pursed her lips in thought for a moment. 'I think it's just over two years.'

'How did they meet?'

'At a dance, I believe.'

'And he worked for a washing machine manufacturer, or so he said.'

'Yes. I never really knew what his exact role was with the company but it must have been fairly important for he always seemed to have a lot of money, so much so that Fran was able to give up work.'

'What did she do?'

'She was in charge of the make-up department at Harrods.'

'Was it a happy marriage?'

'It seemed to be. Walter was away most weeks on business but he'd usually return at the weekend.'

'The business being… washing machine business.'

She nodded. 'I guess so.'

'Well, I can tell you, that it was not. I checked with the firm Klenco where he was supposed to be employed and they told me that they'd had never heard of Walter Clements. His role as a washing machine manager was baloney – a cover for something else.'

'What?'

I shrugged. Here I go with the negatives again. 'I don't know but whatever it was it seems likely it was dodgy, illegal, criminal even.'

'It's all so difficult to take in.'

'Of course it is.'

'What am I to do?'

'With your agreement, I've found you accommodation with an old friend of mine – a thoroughly respectable fellow. You'll be safe there – safer than in an impersonal hotel. My friend Benny will keep an eye on you. The police will want to interview you sometime soon and then we'll take it from there. I'll keep you posted if I make any headway.'

'What are you going to do?'

'It's best if I don't tell you for the moment…'

I got no further as there was a sharp rapping at my office door. My body stiffened slightly. My nerves were still tense after the shooting incident.

'You stay here,' I said, putting my finger to my lips and made my way through to my office, retrieving my revolver from my office desk drawer en route to the door. I needed not have concerned myself, for I could see through the frosted glass of my office door the silhouette of a London bobby, tall helmet and all.

I opened the door and a young, fresh-faced copper with rosy apple cheeks and bright blue eyes raised his gloved hand in salute. He looked like a schoolboy in grown-up clothes. 'I've come on from Superintendent Llewellyn for a certain item of evidence,' he said in a manner not unlike a speak-your-weight machine.

I grinned. 'Of course you have. Wait here and I'll get it.' Seconds later, I returned with the knife still wrapped in the strip of silky bed sheet.

I handed it over. 'Here you are, constable. Guard it with your life,' I said lightly with a smile.

'I will indeed. I will indeed, sir,' he replied with stern

earnestness, stowing the weapon inside a leather bag. With another salute, he left. I closed the door giving a light chuckle. Ten years ago that could have been me: an eager, awkward but serious-minded copper. Where would I have been now in the police hierarchy if it had not been for that blasted accident that robbed me of my eye? Could I have risen like David to the heights of Superintendent? I doubt it. There was always a touch of the maverick about me – always prepared to bend the rules if I felt it necessary. Ah, well, I thought philosophically, perhaps things had worked out as they should have done.

When I returned to the sitting room, I found that Susan had curled up foetus-like on the sofa and was fast asleep. No doubt the drama and the trauma of the last few hours had exhausted the poor thing and her ragged mind had helped her to escape from reality for a while. Who was I to wake her now? I would let her sleep a while. It would do her good.

I sat opposite the sleeping beauty and lit a cigarette. Sleeping beauty she was indeed, with a lovely, slightly tilted nose, full cupid lips, flawless skin and a tumble of honey-coloured hair. Susan Kershaw had all the qualities of a film starlet, but it was more than that attracted me to her. She had an aura of intelligence which shone brightly from her pale blue eyes. Clever women have always been a weakness of mine. For a second, I was tempted to lean forward and stroke her cheek, but an inner voice told me that was totally inappropriate. Although it was quite a while since I had held a woman in my arms and felt the warmth of a passionate embrace, this was not the time for the amorous side of my nature to assert itself. She was, in essence, a client by proxy and in a very stressed state with unstable emotions. It would be criminal to make any romantic advances in such a situation and besides, she was at least ten years younger than me. I sucked hard on my cigarette and banished all such thoughts. Sometimes I can be an idiot.

Susan slept for just over an hour – three cigarettes' worth, in fact. It gave me the opportunity to make another phone call. This one was to Briggsy, another contact at the Yard. Not as high up the police ladder as David, but one that had proved invaluable on many occasions, and I hoped this would be one of them.

On returning to my seat by the fire, Susan began to stir. Her eyes flickered open and I could see that for a few seconds she wondered where on earth she was. Pulling herself up into a sitting position, her features darkened as she remembered all the bleak moments that had occurred that day. The frown on her forehead deepened but as she looked across at me, she attempted a faint smile. 'Sorry, she said softly. 'I went out like a light.'

'No need to apologise. You needed that nap.'

'It's going to take some time for me to adjust to things. When I woke in my flat in Brighton this morning, everything was so ordinary. I was going to make a trip up to London to stay with my sister – just a bit of moral support. And then…' Her eyes moistened and she bit her lip as she fought back her emotions.

'I know,' I said, reaching out and touching her arm gently. 'And I wish I could say something to make things better. It is going to be tough for a while, I'm afraid, but I'll do all I can to help.'

'You've been very kind. I am so sorry I attacked you.'

I grinned sheepishly. 'Oh, not that again. Consider yourself fully exonerated. Now if you feel up to it, we'll make a move to your new quarters.'

We travelled by taxi, and during the journey, I explained all about Benny, his cafe and our relationship. 'He's like the father I never had,' I said, knowing I would never admit that fact to him. Despite his sometimes crusty exterior, he has a heart of gold. 'You will be in very good caring hands with him,' I assured her, 'and I'll be around a great deal of time to make sure you're safe. So there's no need to fret. With both the police and me on the job, I feel sure it won't be long before we see results and get to the bottom of this rotten business.' I was lying, of course, about this final sentiment. All I could see was a large brick wall facing me in this case. Maybe there were a few loose bricks but that thought gave me little hope and encouragement.

When we arrived at Benny's Café, he was on the verge of closing for the day. He just had one customer who was lingering over tea and a toasted teacake. Benny greeted Susan as though

50

she were his long lost daughter. To her surprise and embarrassment, he threw out his arms and embraced her.

'So good to see you, my dear,' he cried extravagantly. 'Any friend of Johnny's is most welcome here.'

I hadn't told Benny in our phone conversation the full story. For his own sake, as well as mine, he didn't need to know. Missing husbands, murdered wives and a shooting incident would have both shocked and delighted him. Given the opportunity, Benny had a wonderful way of interfering in my affairs. This case was too dangerous for me to give him any information which would prompt him to don his Sherlock Holmes hat, acting as though he was my partner and guardian angel. He'd done it before and caused me problems, despite always meaning well. Besides, this was a dangerous business and I needed to keep the old fellow out of harm's way. I had simply informed him that Susan was connected with a case I was involved in and had lost her sister in tragic circumstances. I stressed that was all he needed to know and must not, under no circumstance, question her further when I wasn't around. 'No matter how kind and subtle your interrogation, you will only upset Susan – so stum, Benny, stum!' I'd insisted on my phone call.

'Of course,' he'd said. 'You can rely on me. Discretion is my middle name.' I didn't comment; that wasn't the middle name I used for him.

'You're very kind,' Susan said, recovering from the embrace.

'Now, I expect you are hungry. How would cottage pie, mushy peas and a mug of strong tea sound?'

Susan looked at me for guidance.

'Sounds like a good idea,' I said, 'but perhaps you'd like to show Susan her room first.'

'Of course. Come this way young lady. It's nothing grand but quite cosy.'

Benny led Susan to the back of the café, through a door and up the stairs to his living quarters, where the spare room was situated. I had used it myself on occasion and knew Benny would have prepared it for his new guest with care, ensuring it was fresh, neat and tidy.

I took this opportunity of availing myself of Benny's telephone. After four insistent rings, a gravelly voice responded at the other end. 'Arthur Briggs,' it said sharply.

'Hello, Briggsy. It's Johnny Hawke here. Did you manage to dig out that information I asked for?'

Briggsy chuckled. 'You're a bugger, Johnny. You treat me like your little factotum. The only time you call is when you want something.'

'Darling, don't let's quarrel,' I joshed. 'You know I care for you deeply.'

Briggsy gave his cement mixer guffaw. 'Now don't start giving me ideas.' He laughed again.

In my mind, I could picture Briggsy at the other end of the line in his cramped office in Scotland Yard. He was a chubby fellow, to say the least, and no doubt he was hunched over his desk, receiver in hand, wearing an open-necked shirt, the buttons of which were straining hard across his ample chest in readiness to fly off in all directions. There would be a mug of tea and a piece cake or sandwich within easy reach. I smiled at this image, which I had no doubt was an accurate one.

'What have you found out?' I asked.

'The number you gave me is registered to a Parkinson's Garage, a repair and hire outfit in Tottenham. Arrowsmith Road. Will that do you?'

'It will do me very nicely. Brilliant, Briggsy. I owe you a pint.'

'At my reckoning for all the information I supplied you with over the years, you owe me a barrel of beer at least.' He chuckled gently this time.

I returned the chuckle, thanked him heartily and bid him farewell.

Slender as it was, it was a lead. I gave myself a metaphorical pat on the back. Despite the shock and tension of the moment when that car had roared into life and the gun had appeared through the passenger window outside the Clements' house, I'd had the presence of mind to make a mental note of the registration number. Well, I am a professional, after all.

Benny came back into the room. 'She seems like a nice girl.

She's not in any serious trouble is she?' he said.

'Not the sort you might be thinking off,' I said, pointedly. 'She just needs to keep her head down for a few days. There may well be some unpleasant people seeking her.'

Benny emitted one of his quiet trademark groans. 'You thought after the war, the nastiness would go away.'

'You OK with her staying here?'

He nodded. 'Of course. I'll get her some food now. She looks a little on the thin side. Needs building up. Do you want some, too?'

'No, I'm fine. I've got a little errand to carry out. I'll pop back later this evening to wish you both a good night.'

'A little errand, eh…? I know you and your little errands. He stepped forward and touched my arm. 'Take care, Johnny. Take care.'

'I always do,' I said with a smile as I headed for the door.

CHAPTER NINE

It was late afternoon when a large man in a heavy tweed overcoat entered the office of Superintendent David Llewellyn at Scotland Yard. He hadn't knocked or been ushered in by another officer; he had just walked in. *Barged in, more like*, thought David, as he looked up from the case file he was studying with some surprise and a little annoyance. Who the hell was this interloper? No one just waltzed into his office unannounced.

The intruder was a beefy man of around fifty, with fierce bulging brown eyes which peered out from beneath two dark bushy eyebrows. He stood before David's desk without saying a word but there was an aura of menace about him that made the Scotland Yard man succumb to a sense of unease.

'Who are you and what do you want?' David found himself saying.

Without responding verbally, the man reached into his inside coat pocket and produced a small blue card which he held forward briefly so that David could inspect it. He saw that each card had a photograph of the owner and some figures and writing, but the card was withdrawn and placed back in the man's coat pocket before he had a chance to scrutinise it closely.

'What is all this,' he growled, what little patience he had evaporating.

'National Security, Superintendent,' said the man in a monosyllabic fashion. 'We need to talk.'

After he had left the safe house, Walter Clements had known his task now was to vanish. Not only were the police after him, but Number One and his cronies would be hot on his heels as well. That sandwich image stuck in his mind. It would be a case of capture or elimination – neither prospect pleased him. He was *persona non grata in extremis*. His ultimate goal was to reach the continent and lose himself there, taking on a new identity, but he knew he could not get there by the usual channels –

airports and ferry ports would be watched by both parties and he wouldn't stand a chance of escaping their notice. He knew what he must do but he reasoned that he ought to lie low for a few days away from London while the heat lessened before he made his move. And he knew exactly where he would go.

CHAPTER TEN
From the journal of Johnny Hawke

Despite my dwindling funds, I splashed out on another taxi. I was surprised how quickly Mrs Clements' fee of twenty pounds was disappearing. However, I just didn't fancy travelling all the way to Hammersmith by tube and then search for Arrowsmith Avenue in the dark. My cab driver, with all his knowledge, could take me directly there. And he did.

Dusk was now seeping into the sky. The September evenings were closing in rapidly. As old Willie Shakespeare has it: 'summer's lease has all too short a date'. Arrowsmith Avenue was a long, meandering thoroughfare with a mixture of buildings ranging from a stretch of reasonably tidy semi-detached houses with neat little gardens and well-cut hedges, to a row of shops and a small factory manufacturing heating equipment. However, there seemed to be no sign of Parkinson's Garage. I was beginning to think that maybe Briggsy had got his facts wrong. I passed a patch of spare ground where a few lads were kicking a ball about in the gloom. They shimmered like frantic silhouettes against the darkening azure sky, their high-pitched yelps filling the quiet of the evening like the cries of strange birds. I approached them and asked if they knew where the garage was.

'Yeah, mate,' said one. 'It's right down at the end of the road. Hope you're not a bill collector 'cause the owner's likely to fill your arse with buckshot.'

His comrades laughed at this response as though they regarded it as one of the wittiest things they had ever heard. And, of course, it may have been.

I chuckled, too, to keep them on my side. 'And how do you know that?'

'Cos he's my dad.' His cronies guffawed once more.

'Lucky then I'm not a bill collector.' I said and gave a cheery wave as I set forth again before there was any more opportunity for backchat.

So, I pondered, this Parkinson fellow was a family man, albeit an aggressive one, with apparent money worries if he was in the process of rebuffing bill collectors in a rough manner. Or maybe the kid was just joshing. I wondered how involved in this Clements business Parkinson was. Had he just hired the car out innocently to two homicidal thugs – cash in hand, no questions asked – or was there more to it than that? Had he, for instance, been one of the fellows in the car? He might even have been the one with the gun. If his loutish offspring was to be believed he did have a weapon – one that fired buckshot. Patience, old lad, I told myself as I made my way towards the far end of Arrowsmith Avenue, all will be revealed in a short time.

Eventually, I came upon Parkinson's Garage. Annoyingly, it was the last property on the road before it joined a T junction. It was just my luck that I'd approached the premises from the wrong end of the avenue. Ah, well, Johnny, I told myself, you're here now. There was a rambling prefabricated building set back from the road with a corrugated roof and before it was a small forecourt which contained five second-hand cars. They were for sale, with their prices displayed prominently on the inside of the windscreen. The cars were cheap but looked in reasonable condition. Not for the first time, I thought that it was time I indulged in buying a little car, but getting around London on foot, by tube and taxi was, in the end, more convenient than being your own chauffeur, and where the hell would I garage the brute?

I wandered around the cars, giving them the once and indeed the twice over. Disappointingly, the one with the registration number I remembered was not there. Maybe it was inside the building or around the back – if there was a 'round the back.'

The place was in darkness and there was no sign of anyone about. *Business closed for the day*, I thought, or rather hoped.

I made my way down the side of the premises to the rear and sure enough, there was indeed a 'round the back'. It was a small tarmacked area, where I discovered a pick-up truck and two piles of old tires and a rusty oil drum.

There was a door and a window in the back wall. I gazed in at the window. It was grimy and had a series of bars fixed against it. All was gloom inside. Peering through the glass, I couldn't make out a thing.

The door, of course, was locked, but I retrieved my handy burgling tool and began work. It was to no avail. This lock was not playing ball. When skill fails, one always has to rely on brute force. I looked around for a brick or a large stone, but couldn't find one. Then, in the grey light, I observed a tyre lever by the stack of old tyres. That might well do the trick, if a tad noisy, I thought. Slipping the thin end of the lever into the gap between the door and the wall, I used it rather like a jemmy. Exerting as much force as I could muster, I pulled hard on the lever. After about thirty seconds of concentrated effort, the wood of the door gave a satisfactory groan. It wasn't long before there was an even more pleasing sound of splintering wood. A few more violent wrenches and the door surrendered and slipped open.

Still holding the lever, I stepped inside and took my bearings. It was a cavernous place and gloomy, the only illumination coming from the fading daylight that filtered through the grimy windows, and that was disappearing fast. I knew I couldn't turn on the light – even if I could locate the switch. I had no intention of advertising my presence. In the centre of the area was a ramp positioned over an inspection pit. There was a small van hoisted up on the platform. On the ground below I spotted a large torch. It provided a very pleasing discreet band of light which would aid my investigations.

As I swung the beam around, it landed upon a blackboard fixed to the wall behind the door. Six car registration numbers had been chalked there. With some surprise, I realised that I recognised one of those numbers. It belonged to the car outside the Clements house whose occupants had made a murderous attack on me and Susan. That registration confirmed the fact. Opposite the number plate, the word 'OUT' been appended followed by an asterisk. This suggested that the car had not been returned by the would-be assassins, or that that Parkinson hadn't brought his chalked record up to date. It was a possibility.

Beyond the pit, there were three cars parked in a somewhat

haphazard fashion. I decided to check on the off chance that one of these was the one I was after. As the beam picked out the registration plates I could see that I was out of luck. The car was definitely 'OUT'. As I approached the last vehicle, I saw a dark shape inside, a bulky object draped over the steering wheel. I shone the torch on the thing and then gasped. It was a man, slumped forward, his head resting on the dashboard, his hand on the ignition key as though he had been trying to start up the engine before being struck down. Quickly, I wrenched open the door of the car and as I did so, the man's body slid sideways into my arms. It did not take me long to acknowledge that the fellow was dead. His limp body and ashen skin were good indicators, but not as much as the rather nasty bullet wound at the side of his head. The congealed blood glistened eerily in the torchlight.

I lifted the body from the car and laid it down on the ground, shining the torch on his face. He was a man who I guessed was in his forties, with plump features and thinning hair which was going grey at the temples. He was dressed in a one-piece overall which suggested to me that he was an employee of Parkinson's Garage. In fact, he may well be Parkinson himself. By the feel of his skin and the stiffness of the body, he had been dead for some time. I felt in his overall pockets, but apart from a packet of cigarettes, a box of matches and a tatty looking rag, there was nothing that revealed his identity.

It was at this point that my thoughts were interrupted by a slight sound behind me. Within seconds my body tensed. Instinctively I knew that there was someone else in the garage and they were very near me. Their presence was tangible. I was just about to turn around when I felt a sharp pain at the back of my head. It was fierce and severe and did it for me. I blacked out before I reached the floor.

When I came to, I was lying where I had fallen, twisted into an undignified heap on the garage floor, my cheek resting in a smear of oil. I reckoned that I had not been out for long and apart from the sharp stabbing pain at the back of my head, I didn't think I had suffered any further damage. As I clambered to my feet I felt the back of my head, my fingers searching for the wound. I felt a neat bump and there was a smear of blood on my fingertips, but it could have been worse. However, I reckoned the headache would stay with me for some time. I gazed around me. There was no sight or sound of my attacker, and then I saw my dead friend. He had not been moved; his features still held in the moment of shock before the bullet penetrated his skull. Looking at the wound again, I reckon I was very lucky just to get a bonk on the bonce.

It was strange, I thought, my mind still reasserting itself after my temporary visit to the unconscious zone, that I could actually see him more clearly now – his face, his clothes, even the interior of the car. Why was this? The lights were not on. The answer soon became obvious. Turning around, I caught sight of the source of this strange illumination. To my horror, I realised that someone had started a fire in the far corner of the garage and it was gaining momentum. The flames were already stretching up to the ceiling and heading my way. No doubt the whole building would be an inferno within a few minutes.

I have a strong aversion to being burned alive. It's just one of my foibles. I knew that I had to high tail it out of there in quick sticks if I didn't want to be singed to death. I gazed down at my dead friend. I could hardly leave him to the mercy of the flames and the police would need the body for all sorts of investigative reasons. He had to come with me. As quickly as I could, I lifted the body up from the floor and hauled him over my shoulder like a slab of meat, which to all intents and purposes, that's what he was now. With my burden in place, I headed for the door. On reaching it, my heart sank. The door was closed and as I tested it, my worst fears were realised. It had been relocked and there appeared to be no tyre lever around this time to come to the rescue. I turned around slowly, the body shifting awkwardly on my shoulder, causing me to stagger sideways. As I steadied myself – my burden wasn't exactly lightweight – I saw that the fire was getting closer. I could feel the waves of heat as they rolled in my direction.

At times like this, my brain goes into free fall, like a man tumbling over a cliff edge who reaches out to whatever shrub or branch he can grab hold of to halt his descent to the rocks below. Metaphorically, I had almost reached the bottom of my descent, jagged rocks in readiness to greet me, when a notion struck me. It was a bit crazy but it was all I had. I raced back to the car as fast I could with my mate over my shoulder, dumped the dead body in the back and slipped into the driver's seat. As I turned the ignition, there was a wall of flame rising up before me, dazzling in its ferocious yellow brightness.

I slammed the car into reverse and spun it around so that it was facing away from the fire and towards the door.

'Hang on to your hat,' I cried to my fellow passenger in the back as I revved up the engine. He wasn't wearing a hat and he was dead – but my utterance somehow gave me some comfort. There was something to share my danger – even if it was a corpse. The car shot forward and I aimed it at the door. As it loomed up before me, I suddenly had grave doubts that I was doing the right thing. Too late now, Johnny, old boy. If the door and the surrounding wall proved to be recalcitrant, it could smash the front end of the car and possibly cause the engine to burst into flames. Then I really would be toast.

The car hit the door and the wall with a shuddering bang, the chassis groaning with the force of it. The door had given way a little but still remained more or less intact. However, there were large cracks around the surrounding area which gave me hope that a second attempt might do the trick. I reversed the car and revved it up once more, ready to give it another go. I was conscious that the flames were already on my tail. Even inside the car, I could feel the force of the heat building around me. Now I know what a baked bean feels like, I mused in my growing hysteria. This was my last chance before the fire overwhelmed the vehicle. The car shot forward and thudded into the wall. I kept my foot down on the accelerator as the bonnet began to bore its way through like some giant blunt drill. With a violent cracking sound and a shower of debris, a jagged aperture appeared in the wall and the car gradually edged its way slowly through into the night air. The engine screamed as the vehicle juddered forward. In a shower of debris which came crashing down on the somewhat dented bonnet, the car pushed its way out of the building.

Once I was free of the workshop, I aimed the car at the wooden fence at the far end of the area and smashed through it on to the road where it skidded to a halt. I turned and looked around. By now, the fire had taken hold of the whole garage, creating a bright orange glow in the evening sky. I realised I had just experienced what thriller writers call 'a narrow escape.'

CHAPTER TWELVE
From the journal of Johnny Hawke

It was nearly midnight when I finally reached the security of Hawke Towers and I climbed wearily up the stairs to my little *pied à terre*. The intervening time between my escape from the garage fire and my return to base had been wearisome. I had driven several miles in the severely injured saloon which boasted a squashed malformed bonnet, severely crumpled mudguards and a damaged front wheel. I felt I was driving the clown's car from Billy Smart's Circus. At any moment, I expected the roof to fly off and a spout of water to issue from the bonnet. Eventually, with a painful whimper and a manic hiss of steam, the poor old car gave up the ghost. Luckily there was a telephone box not a hundred yards away. It was from here that I made two phone calls. The first was to Benny to check up on Susan.

'Oh, she's fine, Johnny,' came the familiar voice in tinny tones down the line. 'She's been an angel, helping me in the café to wash up and set out the tables for the morning rush.'

I couldn't help but smile. This was a perfect arrangement for the old schemer. A pretty girl about the place, sharing his chores and not having to pay her.

'She's just gone up to her room now, Johnny. Should I call her? Do you want a word?'

'No, that's fine. If she's OK, don't disturb her. I'm just checking that all is well.'

'Yes, yes, all is well. And is all well with you?'

I gazed back at the hissing wreck of the car and touched the wound on my head. 'Yes, all is well with me. I'll pop in early tomorrow to see her.'

'You do that, my boy.'

'Night, night. Sleep well,' I crooned before replacing the receiver.

Next, I dialled 999 and gave information about the fire and the dead man in an abandoned vehicle. I avoided passing on any of my personal details, much to the annoyance and distress of the operator on the end of the line. I had enough on my plate without getting involved in a case of murder and arson. I was sure I would learn the identity of the dead man once that had been established by the police. It would be then my task to see where he fitted in this increasingly complicated jigsaw puzzle that I had set myself to solve.

As I entered my darkened office, I knew there was someone there. Call it a sixth sense, or the fierce familiarity I had with that lonely room. I was used to the emptiness of it. Another body in the space changed its subtle dynamics. As I closed the door softly, I wished heartily that my revolver was not nestling in my desk drawer. How bloody foolish of me not to have it about my person. Cautiously, I moved forward into the room and then a voice addressed me out of the darkness.

'You're out of whisky,' it said. 'Very remiss of you.'

I clicked on the light to see David Llewellyn sitting in my chair at my desk holding a glass of what was obviously the last of my Johnnie Walker.

'What are you doing here?' I asked, the words emerging more brusquely than intended.

'A fine welcome. A virtually empty whisky bottle and a gruff reception.'

Despite myself, I grinned. 'I'm sorry, but it's been a rather fraught evening and I'm not in the best of tempers. Let me start again. Hello David, to what do I owe this unexpected pleasure…?'

My friend leaned forward on the desk, his relaxed features darkening. 'There have been serious developments on the Clements case,' he said.

Tell me about it, I thought, as the images of the dead man and the blazing garage meshed for a fleeting moment in my mind. With a sigh, I slipped into the client's chair and extracted a cigarette from my case. If I couldn't have a scotch, an infusion of tobacco would have to suffice.

'I had a visit at the Yard late afternoon from a certain individual. A Security chappie. Bit of a bully boy. So hush bloody hush he didn't even confirm which particular department he was from, but he was certainly a top spy guy. He had no qualms about giving me orders and instructions as though I was some wet behind the ears PC just out of Hendon.'

'Spy guy?'

'Espionage. Apparently, your Mr Clements was actually employed at the War Office.'

'Really? There are no washing machines there.'

'Right. He's been a naughty boy, supplying information to the enemy.'

'Which particular enemy? There seem to be so many now.'

'The spy chappie informed me it was the Russians. Our security boys latched on to Clements' nefarious activities but he managed to slip through their net before they could apprehend him.'

'Careless of them.'

'So, now he's on the run.'

'You don't think his masters will arrange for him to be shipped to Russia?'

David shrugged and shook his head gently. 'The spy chappie intimated that he's slipped through their fingers as well. He has done a runner, frightened of what they might do to him and equally of the fate that British justice meets out to traitors'.

I took a long drag on my cigarette and then watched the smoke spiral towards the ceiling as I digested this information. 'So, now he has been exposed as a spy he is no longer any use to the Ruskies and as a result, Mr C is expendable. He's not destined for a cosy flat overlooking Gorky park, but rather a bullet in the head.'

'That's about it.'

A little lightbulb clicked on in my brain, exposing a set of new thoughts prompted by David's recital. 'So it is possible that the Russians were responsible for Mrs Clements' death.'

'It is very possible. Just making sure that she couldn't blab to the authorities.'

'But surely she didn't know he was a spy. She thought he sold washing machines for God's sake. Why else would she come to me if she knew what he was really doing? It doesn't make sense.'

'Yes, I reckon she was an innocent party in all this. They were probably just being thorough. You know what these bastards are like for rubber stamping everything. But there is a further complication.'

'Of course, there had to be. And what is that?'

'Clements has a microfilm of the utmost importance. His last grand hurrah was to copy files which apparently if they fell into the Ruskies' hands would be disastrous for us.'

'And he is still in possession of this microfilm.'

'So I was led to believe.'

'By this spy guy?'

David nodded.

'And what is on the microfilm?'

'He wouldn't divulge that to me, I'm afraid. He just gave the impression it was pretty high profile stuff.'

'Hey ho. So now we have to find Mr C before the Ruskies do,' I observed with a grimace.

'Yes. That is the scenario that was presented to me. But I was told that the whole matter was now out of my hands.'

'What do you mean?'

'I was told to back off – to stay out of the matter altogether. It is now being managed by the national security boys. Scotland Yard has to withdraw.'

'That's crazy. Surely it's a case of all hands to the pump.'

'Apparently, the case is a delicate one. Protocol and all that. On the surface, we must not appear to be beastly to the Russians – as Noel Coward almost said - while at the same time we have to be rooting out their rotten agents embedded in this city. It would seem that they consider the police as too ham-fisted and too bound by regulations to deal the matter. We cannot be trusted to proceed with sufficient delicacy. How did he put it? We were not "surreptitious enough."'

'Bollocks!'

David chuckled. 'You were always an eloquent fellow. Bollocks, indeed. My exact thought. This spy chap made me feel like Mr Plod. It's like being sent off the field by an overbearing ref for no good reason at all.'

'Surely you're not giving up?'

'Officially, of course, I am… Smacked buttocks if I don't.'

'Unofficially?'

'I'm staying on the field and giving the ref two fingers. I'm going to find that Clements bastard!'

'Well, you can count on me to help. Technically, it is still my case as well.'

'That's why I am here. I will need a rogue man in the field to help out.'

'A rogue man?'

'You know what I mean. Someone who is not bound by rules and responsibilities to a higher authority. A free agent.'

'I prefer the term "free agent" to a "rogue man" – that makes me sound like a Neanderthal'. I slipped him a quick grim grin. 'Well, now I have things to tell you,' I said, lighting up another cigarette. I recounted in detail my adventures of the night. He sat in the dim light, listening intently, his eyes wide with interest.

'Who do you reckon the dead man is?' he asked when I had ended my spiel.

'Well, he's not Mr C that's for certain. I'd put my money on it being Parkinson, the garage owner. After what you've told me, it would seem that our Russian friends are in the process of eliminating all possible leads in this case. Now that Clements has been found out, they're wiping the slate clean. Anyone who had anything to do with this affair is for the chop.'

'It sounds rather melodramatic, but you could be right. If that is the case, they'll want to do the same to Clements. Not only is he no longer any use to them as a spy in the camp, but he is a threat to them and their covert organisation if our boys get hold of him. Apart from recovering the microfilm, he'll certainly have secrets to spill. That's another reason that it is imperative that we get our hands on this fake washing machine salesman before they do.'

I nodded in agreement.

'He's on the run now and no doubt headed for some bolt hole. Somewhere that is not going to be easy to find,' said David wearily, stifling a yawn. The long day was catching up with him; I knew how he felt. 'Where the hell do we start?'

I thought for a moment. 'I might have an idea of how to proceed.'

'How?'

I placed my finger to the side of my nose and tapped it. 'Rogue man has his methods. I'll reveal all after I've given it a try.'

'No secrets now, Johnny, this is too serious for silly games.'

'Don't worry. I'll keep you informed when there is something significant to report. In the meantime, you find out the identity of that dead man I left in the battered saloon and let me know.'

'Of course.' With a fatigued sigh, he rose from his chair. 'I'd better get home now, but we must keep our allegiance under wraps. Don't visit me at the Yard. Just call, say hello and we'll arrange a rendezvous.'

'That suits me.'

David Llewellyn gave me a wry smile, tugged his trilby into a jaunty slouch and let himself out.

I sat in my chair for a while, thinking hard and wishing I had another bottle of whisky stashed away somewhere.

CHAPTER THIRTEEN
From the journal of Johnny Hawke

Next morning, after what I had learned the night before, the world seemed even more gloomy than usual and it took me quite a while to crank up any enthusiasm to face the challenge of the day. I did quite a bit of talking to myself, desperately trying to rally my spirits while I shaved, my one eye staring back at me from the mirror in an accusative fashion. Get your act together, Hawke, it seemed to suggest angrily. However, the glimmer of a notion of how to proceed in this complicated affair that I'd nurtured the previous evening seemed to have lost its original tenuous glimmer altogether.

I breakfasted at Benny's with Susan as my dining companion. Nosily, old Benny hovered in the background when kitchen duties allowed, no doubt waiting to catch a snatch of conversation in order to work out what the hell was going on. What mystery surrounded her, and more particularly, was Johnny in the process of acquiring another girlfriend. Benny was an out and out romantic, and nothing would have made him happier than to see me settled down with a lovely wife and a baby nestling my lap. If the truth be known, this pipe dream would suit me also, but I was fairly sure that it wasn't going to happen.

Susan appeared remarkably cheerful considering her plight, but her pale face still spoke of her strain and fatigue, and the redness of her eyes gave evidence that she had been crying. I told her nothing of the recent developments in the case. There was no need at this juncture and the news would upset her all the more. However, she was eager to know what was happening with the investigation and when she could expect to be interviewed by the police regarding her sister's death.

'I've arranged for the police to leave you alone for a while,' I told her. 'I have contacts at Scotland Yard,' I said with a smile and a rather amateurish wink. 'I said I'll pass on any information I get from you that I think may be useful to them.

But I will tell you this, they think that whoever took a shot at us yesterday and probably murdered your sister, are now after Walter and he is most likely on the run.'

She shook her head, bewildered. 'Why? What has he done? Who are these people?'

'I don't know,' I lied, my eyes averting her gaze. 'But I think you might be able to help me.'

'How?'

'Well,' I said slowly, 'can you tell me all you knew about Walter Clements.'

'I thought I already had,' she said, somewhat nonplussed.

'There must be some other details – small things that may seem insignificant to you but in the end, could give us a lead. You said you were not keen on the fellow.'

She nodded. 'He never seemed relaxed in my company, and I must say that I never felt easy with him. I wouldn't say he was brusque, just stiff and reserved.' Suddenly she smiled, 'Except that one time when he got rather squiffy.'

I leaned forward and touched her hand. 'Tell me about it.'

'I'd come up to London for the weekend. On the Saturday night, the three of us had gone to the first house at the pictures and then to the pub. Walter drank rather too much beer and when we got back home, he started on the whisky. Frances was a little merry, too, and she went off to bed early. I tried to follow but Walter insisted I had a whisky with him. He was rambling a little by this time and I was eager to leave and get to bed but he wasn't having any of it. "Don't leave me alone," he said. "I hate being alone. I've been alone most of my life," he said, more to himself than to me. I thought it was a strange thing to say. Here he was, married to my sister. How could he be alone? Then suddenly, he started talking about his childhood. "My dad died when I was two," he said, the drink now making him maudlin. "I had a lonely childhood," he went on. "My mum was good but she had the shop to run and had little time for me". I asked him what kind of shop it was. "A sweetie shop," he said. "I suppose it could be seen as an Aladdin's cave to a young boy, all those shelves packed with lovely sweeties – but I really wasn't interested in them. Never had a sweet tooth.'''

'Did you ask him where this sweet shop was?'

She nodded. 'He told me it was in Rye.'

'So that was where he was born?'

Susan shrugged. 'I guess so. It was the only time that I saw a soft vulnerable side to him, but it was mainly because of the drink. To be honest, Johnny, I was embarrassed and wanted to get to my room.'

'Did he say more?'

She shook her head. 'He muttered something that I couldn't hear and then he just drifted off into sleep.'

'Do you think he loved Frances?'

'I honestly don't know. They appeared to rub along OK, but as things have turned out and after what you've told me, he seemed to be living some kind of double life.'

Bullseye! Give the lady a prize.

'Yes,' I said softly. 'Well, perhaps the answer lies in a sweet shop in Rye.'

'Really? You think he might have gone there?'

'It's a possibility and it's the only rather fragile thread I have. I have to give it a go.'

'You mean you're going down to Rye?'

'Yes.'

'Then I'm coming with you.'

'Oh, no you're not. I can't risk that; there may be danger involved. You'll be a lot safer staying in the café.'

'I insist, Johnny. I can't spend another day just twiddling my thumbs here. I want to get to the bottom of this mystery just as much as you. If you refuse to take me with you, I'll go on my own.' She leaned forward and grabbed my hand. 'I mean it,' she said. Her eyes told me that she was deadly serious.

In less than an hour, we were boarding a train at St Pancras for Rye. The morning rush had ceased and we managed to get a compartment to ourselves. I could tell Susan was pleased and relieved to actually be doing something to sort out the mystery of her sister's death, rather than just waiting for news. Her features had already brightened and a little colour had returned to her cheeks. She accepted a cigarette and seemed the most

71

relaxed that I had seen her. In one sense, she was a vulnerable creature, but in her determination to accompany me to Rye I had observed that she had strong independent streak. The more I saw of this girl, the more I liked her. In fact, the more I grew fonder of her.

'So what do you do in Brighton?' I asked.

'Oh, nothing exciting. I work in as a secretary for a solicitor, Mr Rosebury. He's a sweetie. When I asked him if I could take a few days off as my sister needed company in London because her husband had gone missing, he was most sympathetic and said I could take as long as I liked.'

'When did you move to Brighton?'

Her eyes flickered uneasily. 'A couple of years ago. I moved down to be near my boyfriend. He'd got a job as car salesmen there. We were planning to get married.' She paused and gazed out of the carriage window. 'It didn't work out.'

'I'm sorry.'

'Yes, so was I, but I guess these things happen. He... he found someone else. Simple as that. Anyway, I liked Brighton. It's a very lively town, and there's the sea and the beach, so I stayed.'

'Is there a new boyfriend?' I asked, and I really shouldn't have.

She shook her head and gave a wry smile. 'Once bitten...'

There followed an awkward silence. Then she stubbed her half-smoked cigarette out in the metal tray as though to indicate a line had been drawn under that topic of conversation and gave me a strained smile. 'So, Mr Detective, what are your plans when we arrive in Rye?' she said brightly, channelling the conversation elsewhere.

'Well, it's a fairly small town; there can't be many shops that only sell sweets – a real old fashioned sweetie shop. If it was in business when Clements was a boy it's been around for a while. We might have to tramp around a bit and ask a few of the locals.'

'And if you find it? What then?'

I grinned. 'That's when I have to rely on my instincts – play it by ear as they say.'

It was clear from Susan's expression that she did not have the artifice to hide her surprise. I could understand. No doubt she was wondering what kind of detective was this chap who had no real plan of action. She wasn't to know that is how I approached all my cases – relying on my gut reaction to events. Over the years, this fragile technique had worked on the whole, with one or two very unpleasant exceptions over which my mind is always quick to draw a thick veil.

Some two hours later, we stepped off the train in the quaint seaside town of Rye and our investigations were about to begin.

CHAPTER FOURTEEN

Walter Clements studied his reflection in the bathroom mirror. He approved of what he saw and gave himself a tight smile. It wasn't a smile of merriment, rather it was one of smug satisfaction. The Walter Clements of old had been transformed: the neat moustache had gone and the wavy hair had been cut very short and dyed blonde. The addition of a pair of wire-rimmed glasses completed the transformation. *I look like a rather stern German general, the sort portrayed in the British films*, he mused and the smile broadened. He was tempted to give himself a 'Heil Hitler' salute but resisted the urge. Now he was ready to face the world as his new self or, more precisely, hide from the world. His next task was to get to Europe, where he was sure he would have no difficulty in disappearing and beginning a new life.

The shop bell tinkled gently as a man and woman entered. It was shortly after nine in the morning. The owner, whose head was only just visible above the counter, was busy knitting. At the sound of the bell, she looked up and observed the two customers silhouetted against the bright light shining in through the glass in the shop door; a stout woman and a tall willowy man. Putting her knitting to one side, she rose to her feet and leaned over the counter.

'Good morning,' she said briskly. 'May I help you?'

The woman stepped forward. She was overly made up and bore an unpleasant expression on her fleshy pugnacious features. She wore bright dangly earrings that glinted in the dim light.

'Mrs Clements?' she said, her voice harsh with a sinister threatening edge.

The owner stiffened. 'Who wants to know?'

In response, the man joined the woman near the counter. 'We are from Scotland Yard...' he said, his tone just as unpleasant as the woman's.

'Are you, by Jove? And I'm the Queen of Sheba,' came the brusque reply.

The man reached into his inside pocket and brought out a plastic wallet which contained a small printed document with his photograph. 'My credentials. If you'd care to inspect them.'

'Yes I would,' said the owner, holding out her hand. The old woman scrutinised them carefully, although she was fairly certain that they were fake. She handed the wallet back without comment and turned her gaze to the woman. 'And yours,' she said, thrusting out her hand. With an exasperated sigh, the woman dipped into her handbag and produced a similar wallet which received the same scrutiny.

'So, are you going to buy some sweeties? There is a special offer on bonbons this week; six ounces for the price of four.'

'We are not here to buy sweeties…' began the man.

'Really? But this is a sweet shop.'

'We are here to talk about your son.'

The old lady raised her eyebrows. 'Are you now?'

'Yes. Is he here?'

The response to this question was a raucous guffaw. 'If he was he'd get the rough end of my tongue, I can tell you. For your information, I haven't seen the bastard for five years. He just upped and left with a week's takings and he never came back. Good riddance.'

'You haven't seen him in the last week?' asked the woman.

'I didn't think they employed deaf and stupid cops at Scotland Yard. I just said I haven't set eyes on the bastard for five years. Can't be plainer than that.'

'In that case, we need to search the premises.'

'Do you now? Well, you'll be needing a warrant for that, won't you?'

The man placed his hand in his jacket pocket. 'I have one here.'

And it's as real as your credentials, no doubt, thought the old lady. 'Oh, do as you please,' she growled, 'but you'll be wasting your time.'

'We'll be the judge of that.'

'Very well then. You can look but you can't touch. I've got

some very nice ornaments about the place. I don't want any to slip inadvertently in your pocket.'

The man and woman exchanged a brief glance.

'I'll stay here and keep an eye on her,' the woman said.

The man nodded and moved around the counter and disappeared into the living quarters at the back of the shop.

'Are you sure I can't tempt you to some sweeties?' asked the old lady.

'I'm sure,' came the terse reply.

'Scotland Yard, eh? That sounds serious. What's the rascal been up to now?'

The woman did not reply and so the old lady gave a shrug and returned to her knitting. Very shortly, there came sounds from above as the man investigated the bedrooms.

'I hope your assistant isn't mucking about with my things up there. Don't know why you can't take my word for it. My son is not here. If he was, I'd gladly tell you – but, as I've already said, I haven't seen him for five years.'

The woman who claimed to be from Scotland Yard said nothing.

Five minutes later, the man emerged from the back of the shop. He shook his head. 'Nothing,' he said softly.

The old lady chuckled. 'I told you.'

'Have you any idea where Walter Clements might be?'

The old lady shrugged. 'He could be in Tahiti or Tottenham, I don't know and I don't care.'

The man and the woman turned towards the door.

'Have you done then… with your enquiries?' The old lady chuckled again. 'You could at least have bought some sweeties, some humbugs to suck while you make your way back to Scotland Yard. I reckon humbugs would suit you two.'

Her visitors left without making a response. The shop bell tinkled sweetly, announcing their departure.

Left alone, all humour and ease evaporated from the old woman's features. She waited for a few minutes before moving and then, with speed that belied her years, she rushed to the door, gazed out on to the street beyond to make sure her visitors had gone. With a satisfied grunt, she slipped the catch on the door and swung around the 'open' sign to 'closed'. Then, she hurried into the hall beyond the shop premises and pulled back the heavy Persian rug that was positioned there, exposing a trap door with a rusty iron ring set into it.

Using both hands, she hauled the trap door open to reveal a set of wooden stairs leading downstairs.

'Don't panic. It's only me,' she called, as she made her way down. Passing through a curtain at the bottom, she entered a brightly lit chamber, one that had been used in the war when the bombers came over dropping their load on the town. It was now kittled out as bijou living quarters with a bed, washbasin, chest of drawers and a commode. Lying on the bed was a tall fellow with short blonde hair and wearing a pair of wire-rimmed glasses. As his mother entered, he swung his legs over the edge of the bed and leaned forward. His face wore an anxious expression but he did not speak.

'You were right. They have come looking. They've just been. Said they were from Scotland Yard,' Mrs Clements said.

'A likely story. Describe them to me, Ma.'

She did so, but her details were sketchy for the lighting in the shop was dim and for the most part, they had kept to the shadows.

'Did the woman wear long dangling golden earrings? Ostentatious trinkets.'

Mrs Clements nodded.

Walter smiled. 'That would be Olga. Her companion was most likely Basil – tall fellow, thin. They work in tandem.'

Mrs Clements nodded again. 'Who are they?'

'The cleaners. Any mess and they sort it out.'

'Don't like the sound of that, Wally. I reckon you are the mess in this case…' Before Clements could reply, she held up her hand. 'I don't want to know the details. Whatever you've done, I'm your mother and it's my job to protect you – despite the fact that you look like a German criminal with that yellow stuff on your hair and those Nazi glasses.' She shuddered.

He got his feet and gave her a hug. 'It's still me under this disguise and I love you, darling.'

'And you're going to love me and leave me, aren't you,

Wally?'

'You know I've got to. The buggers are close. I wouldn't put it past them to put a watch on this house. I've got to get away further down the coast. I've got to find a boat that will get me to France. Their appearance here is my cue to go. I'll slip out of here after dark.'

CHAPTER FIFTEEN
From the journal of Johnny Hawke

'Well, there are lots of shops in the town that sell sweets…
but the only one I can think of that is a proper old fashioned
sweet shop is Sweet Dreams on Plover Road, down near the
foreshore.' The red-faced lady in the yellow headscarf raised
her arm and pointed down the hill.

I doffed my hat. 'Thank you', I said graciously. 'That's been
a great help.'

'Not at all, always happy to help a fellow with a sweet tooth
like myself,' she said, chuckling and went on her way.

'So Sweet Dreams it is,' I said. 'Let's seek it out.'

Susan nodded. 'OK, but what then?'

I shrugged. 'I don't know.'

Sweet Dreams was the image of an old fashioned sweet shop,
almost Dickensian in aspect. It had a dusty bow-fronted window
with small panes and a rather faded display of tins, packets and
boxes of chocolates, toffees, fruit gums and various chewy,
sugary items. It had once been colourful, but it had been there
for some time and had lost its freshness and vibrancy, faded by
the coastal sun. A visit there would have been the greatest of
treats during the war, and even today, because of the sugar
rationing of such confectionery it was still something of a
luxury.

'Bull by the horns time,' I said as we approached. 'Let's go
in.

'You want me to come in with you?' asked Susan.

'It might be useful if we catch sight of Walter. I only know
him from his photograph.'

'OK,' she said, taking hold of my hand.

My heart skipped a beat.

The inside of Sweet Dreams was as gloomy and faded as was
the window display, but the air was filled with a very pleasing
sugary aroma. There was an old lady sitting behind the counter

knitting. She glanced up as a little bell above the shop door announced our entrance.

'Good afternoon,' she said without much enthusiasm, as she put down her knitting and rose to her feet. 'What can I get you?'

'Mrs Clements…?' I said cheerily.

Her face froze and she remained silent for some moments.

'It is Mrs Clements, isn't it?' I prompted.

'Who wants to know?'

'A friend of your son, Walter.'

'I know of no friend of Walter's who wears an eye patch.'

'Where is he, Mrs Clements? He is in terrible trouble and I am here to help him.'

'What trouble?'

'I cannot say, but as his mother, I am sure you would want to see him safe. I can help him.'

'I don't know what you're talking about and I'd thank you to leave my shop now.'

Susan moved closer to the counter. 'I am Susan Kershaw, Frances Clements was my sister. She's been murdered and Walter has disappeared.'

From the expression on the old woman's face, I could tell that this information was news to her.

'If you know where Walter is, it would be wise to tell us. It would be best for him and for you,' I said. Then a thought struck me. 'Is he here now?'

The old lady hesitated before she spoke, her face registering a series of thoughts crossing her mind, as though she didn't quite know how to respond.

'I don't know where he is,' she growled eventually.

'You are alone here?'

'Yes, just me and my gobstoppers for company.' She gave a throaty cough which I suppose was meant to be a laugh, but her features remained stern and resolute.

Just then, there was the noise of movement from the back of the shop and what sounded like a door slamming shut. In an instant, Susan had let go of my hand and shot past me, around the side of the counter and through the door beyond that led to the rear of the property. As she did so, she called out, 'Walter!'

at the top of her lungs. I made to follow her, but the woman rushed forward to bar my way. It is not in my nature to slug an old dear in the kisser but on occasion, needs must. I would have done just that had she not grabbed a large sweet jar – full of humbugs, as I recall – and bashed me around the head with it. I saw double and crumpled to the floor. The harpy came at me again but I had enough energy and foresight to slither backwards and avoid the blow. I jumped to my feet and wrestled the heavy jar from her grip and pushed her sideways. She fell against the counter and with a winded sigh slid to the ground.

'He's here, Johnny,' came Susan's voice from beyond and then, to my horror, there was a gunshot.

I ran past the counter through the door into the hallway beyond where I saw Susan lying on the ground.

'My God,' I cried as I knelt by her. 'Are you hurt?'

'He missed me, the bullet went astray,' she muttered.

'Thank heavens,' I said.

'But,' she added, her hand fluttering to her forehead where there was a small trickle of blood, 'he managed to hit me with the butt of the gun'

I leant forward to examine the wound, which did not seem too serious.

'Don't worry about me,' she snapped. 'Quickly, get after him...' She raised her arm to point the way.

She was right. Without a word, I followed her instructions and raced down the corridor. It led to a small kitchen which had a back door. It was swinging open. I ran through, down a path which led to a lane. It was deserted. Clements could have gone either way. I travelled a hundred yards in one direction and then the other. There was no sign of the blighter. It seemed that he had disappeared, or more accurately – escaped.

I made my way back to the shop via the rear entrance. Susan was on her feet now but leaning against the wall.

'How do you feel?' I asked.

'I'll live. He got away then?'

'He turned himself into the invisible man. I'd better go and attend to Old Mother Riley through there. She has a lot to answer for. Are you sure you're OK?'

'A couple of aspirins and I'll be as right as rain.'

Instinctively, I leaned forward and gave her a kiss on the cheek. Immediately, I knew what I had done was a mistake. Before I could gauge her reaction, I moved swiftly into the shop. Mrs Clements was more or less where I'd left her. She had got to her feet but was leaning on the counter, breathing heavily.

'You knew your son was here all the time and you knew that he was a fugitive from the law.'

She screwed her face up into a ferocious scowl of gargoyle dimensions. 'Get lost!' She spat the words out with venom. 'You'll get nothing out of me'.

'Maybe not, but maybe the police will when they arrive.'

'They'll get nothing out of me either. Nothing, I tell you.'

To my mind, there was a kind of irony that this fierce and obstreperous old lady should be in charge of a sweet shop. Here she was, doling out fudge, raspberry creams and other saccharine treats while concealing a sour and bitter nature. I was aware that it was a twisted kind of loyalty to her son that made her this way. He was her baby, her beloved offspring and no matter what he had done, she would protect him, lie for him, bash inquisitive fellows around the napper with a sweet jar, if necessary. In some strange way, I felt sorry for her.

With sluggish movements, she made her way around the corner of the counter and resumed her stool and picked up her knitting as though nothing had happened. It struck me that she was the Madame Defarge of the sweetie shop world. She gazed up at me with contempt, her look telling me that she wasn't going anywhere unless removed by force. This was her shop, her home, her domain and here she would remain – knitting – until the crack of doom or until a burly policeman clapped handcuffs on her and conveyed her to a Black Maria.

I left her to her knit one, purl one activity and located a telephone in the little sitting-room at the back of the shop. I contacted David at Scotland Yard and filled him in on details.

'Well done, Sherlock,' he said. 'Leave things to me. I'll alert the local police to come along and cart the old bag away. In the meantime, is there any hope you can wheedle out of her where her son has gone to now?'

'Do cats have a chance in hell?' I replied. 'She's a strong lady, devoted to sonny boy. Her lips are sealed. If they've got thumb screws and boiling oil down at the local nick they may have better luck – but I doubt it.'

'Pity.'

'Don't despair. I'm sure I can find out where Walter has gone,' I lied. 'Trust me.'

'What? And break the habit of a lifetime, boyo.' He gave a dark chuckle. 'Keep in touch.'

'Will do. Tell your mates down here to hurry to pick up the sweetie lady.'

I replaced the receiver. 'Sweetie lady,' I muttered to myself. 'That's the last thing she is.'

My little reverie was interrupted by a cry from the hall. 'Johnny. Come here quickly.' It was Susan. I could not tell whether she was excited or frightened. *What now?* I thought as I hurried to her summons. I found her in the hall standing before an open trap door. I could see that there was a wooden staircase leading down to what I assumed was a cellar or underground room.

'Look what I found,' said Susan, her eyes alive with excitement.

There was a light switch on the wall by the first step. I switched it on and began to descend. Without hesitation, Susan followed me. What we discovered at the bottom was a very neat room containing a bed and other items which made it a very snug hideaway. 'This must have been used in the war as a kind of bomb shelter,' I said. 'Ideal now for Walter to secrete himself away.'

On the sink, I observed an empty packet of hair dye. I picked it up and examined it. Had our friend gone ash blonde? Susan answered my unspoken thought.

'He had short blonde hair when I saw him – and he'd shaved off his moustache, too. I could tell it was still the old Walter but for those who don't know him, he could easily pass for someone else. I suppose it's like a disguise.'

'Cunning little devil,' I observed, with not a certain amount of chagrin. Another bloody obstacle to contend with. Looking around the room, it was obvious that Walter hadn't been expecting to leave in such a hurry. There were many personal items left here, including a suitcase. He had probably just popped upstairs for something or other, not realising there were hounds on his trail in the property questioning his mother and was caught off guard when he encountered Susan. She was lucky to be alive. If that bullet had not gone astray… It was a thought that I did not want to pursue.

I investigated the suitcase. It contained a couple of shirts and underclothes, along with a sports jacket, a pair of flannel trousers and toiletries. But what caught my attention was a map tucked down the side of the case. It was folded open on the section featuring the south coast. I sat on the bed to study it. Susan sat beside me.

'Look,' I said, excitedly, pointing, 'he's put a black mark here, by Littlehampton.'

'That must be where he's going.'

I nodded. 'It would seem so. A stopping off point on his way to the continent, no doubt. His escape route, if you like.'

'How's he going to get there? I reckon it's over sixty miles or so from here.'

'I don't know, but he'll not try travelling by train, not now he knows we're hot on his trail. He can't afford to be seen on public transport. One thing is certain, we've got to follow him. Once he leaves these shores we've lost him for good.'

'Do you think his mother knows of his plans?'

'I'm not sure. He may well have kept all that information to himself on the principle that the fewer people knew, the better. One thing is for sure, if she does know, she won't spill the beans. She's a tough old boot. The police are not allowed to torture folk in this country and that's the only way they'd get a squeak out of her. And talking of Old Mother Riley, we'd better nip upstairs to keep an eye on her until the police come to take her away.'

Remarkably, when we returned to the shop, the old crone was still seated behind the counter, knitting furiously. While waiting for the police, I took the opportunity to ring David again to alert him to the change in Walter's appearance.

'Clean-shaven and blonde-haired, eh? Cunning bastard.'

'And Susan said that he was wearing what looked like a blue suit and an open-necked white shirt.'

'No overcoat.'

'No, he left in a hurry.'

'OK Johnny, thanks for the update. Keep me in the loop.'

Some ten minutes later, the police arrived in the form of a Detective Sergeant, by the name of Bradley, and two serious-faced constables.

'I've been fully briefed on the matter,' said Bradley with reassuring confidence. 'I had a short but illuminating conversation with Superintendent Llewellyn on the blower. Are you wanting to accompany us to the station with the lady?'

I shook my head. 'No. We have other fish to fry, but if you manage to wring any information out of Mrs Clements make sure you pass it on immediately to the Yard.'

'Of course.'

'He won't get anything out of me, be assured of that,' sneered the old lady, still knitting assiduously.

Bradley approached her cautiously. He could see that she was likely to be a difficult customer. 'Now, madam, are you going to come with me nicely, without restraint or do I have to get one of my men here to handcuff you.'

'You don't need to use force with me, sonny. I'm ready to go if you are, but I'm taking my knitting.' She rose and moved around the counter and made for the door. The two constables parted to allow her passage and suddenly she stopped and turned. 'One little favour,' she said to Bradley. 'I'd like a word in the ear of Mr Eye Patch here before I leave.'

The Detective Sergeant seemed a little surprised by the request, as was I, but he nodded his approval.

The old girl approached and pulled my sleeve so that I bent down in order for her to whisper in my ear. Before she spoke, she gave a little chuckle and then said sotto voce, 'A little information, matey: my son's wife never had a sister.'

CHAPTER FIFTEEN

Sir Jeremy gripped the receiver angrily. Furrows of frustration and anger creased his brow. 'I seem to be surrounded by idiots,' he growled. His rage was steely and threatening. 'First Chapman allows Clements to knock him out and do a runner and now you tell me you've let him slip through your fingers in Rye.'

'The old lady swore that he wasn't there,' came the cringing reply.

'And you believed her? You took her at her word?' Sir Jeremy could hardly contain his fury.

'Well... yes.'

'Imbecile.'

'Sorry, but...'

'I don't allow room for 'buts'. We can't afford them... or tolerate them.'

'Yes, sir.' The voice was now cowed into a timid whisper.

'And now you say the woman has been taken away by the police and Hawke has been to the premises sniffing around?'

'Yes. Olga is in the car parked near the shop, keeping an eye on things.'

'Well, for God's sake make sure Hawke is not aware he's being watched,' he said. 'Follow him. Wherever he goes. It seems he has more perception and initiative than you two put together. With a bit of luck, we can use him to help find Clements. In no way must you harm or hinder Hawke until our man has been located. Just keep on his tail and don't bloody lose him!'

'Yes, sir.'

'I assume the girl is still with him?'

'Yes, sir.'

Sir Jeremy smiled for the first time in a long while. That, at least, is one consolation, but he kept that thought to himself.

'We must retrieve that bloody microfilm. It is essential, and then Clements must be eliminated and on British soil. He must not be allowed to escape to the continent. He carries with him – in his head – too much information about us to be allowed to live. If he or the microfilm falls into the hands of the British authorities… If you fail…' He paused here deliberately for dramatic effect. 'I cannot answer for the consequences. Is that understood?'

'Yes, sir.' The voice was now merely a squeak of which even a mouse would have been ashamed. The implications were clear enough.

'Good.' Sir Jeremy replaced the receiver and retrieved a small cigar from a silver box on his desk. 'Incompetents,' he muttered to himself. If they failed, it would reflect very badly on himself with his masters. He fully realised that the buck stopped at his door. That must not happen. 'At least,' he mused as he inhaled the pungent aroma of the cigar, 'at least I have a joker in the pack.'

Herbert Jenkins slipped another piece of chewing gum between his lips. His mouth was getting dry again and he was tired. Masticating quickly helped to keep him awake. He really should have pulled in off the road for a rest, a nap even, but he just wanted to get to his destination. He was not one for breaking his journey. He liked to leave point A and get to point B as quickly as possible without any breaks or intervals. Once he'd delivered his load, then he could rest and fill his belly with ale and pasties. He held that thought as he chewed the gum and drove on.

As he made his way beyond Rye and out on the road towards Maidstone, he really was feeling weary. He felt his eyelids start to droop, but he was too stubborn to stop and take a rest. He blinked furiously and slipped another piece of gum in his mouth to help keep himself alert. 'I'll get there and in one piece,' he muttered to himself with confidence, although his mind was not so sure. He wound down his window to allow a blast of fresh air to invade the cab and refresh the stale and stultifying atmosphere. As he did so, he saw a figure ahead of him on the roadside, his arm raised high, waving. A hitchhiker – some bloke thumbing a lift.

Usually, he ignored these freeloaders as he considered them, but on this occasion, he thought it might be useful to have a passenger on board. A conversation with a stranger would help him keep awake. Be company for him, anyway, as he pressed down on the brake and pulled in some yards ahead of the man who rushed towards the lorry. Herbert could see him in the wing mirror: a bloke in his late thirties with blonde hair, dressed in a blue suit. He had no luggage and no overcoat. Very odd.

The stranger yanked open the passenger door. He looked like a foreigner – Germanic, with his short blonde hair and steel-rimmed spectacles. However, when he spoke he sounded very English indeed. 'Thanks for stopping,' he said. 'I'm headed towards Littlehampton. Can you take me there or part of the way at least? I'd be very grateful.'

'I can drop you close by. Hop in.'

'That is so good of you,' said the man, clambering into the cab.

Once the door was closed, Herbert Jenkins revved up the engine and set off on the road once more.

CHAPTER SIXTEEN
From the journal of Johnny Hawke

Once the police had left with Old Mother Riley in tow, we locked up the shop and set forth.

'What now?' asked Susan.

'I spotted a garage up the road some way. We may be able to hire a car from them so we can motor to Littlehampton, which is likely to be Walter's next port of call.'

'OK,' she said with enthusiasm. Susan had washed her face and applied some antiseptic she'd discovered in the bathroom to the cut on her forehead. It now appeared no more than a mere scratch. 'With a little extra makeup, I'm as good as new,' she had said. And she was! Pretty as a picture once more.

My mind had been somewhat in turmoil after what Ma Clements had told me: 'my son's wife never had a sister.' Was it true, or was the old bat just winding me up? She was just the type to spill out a prize porky as a curtain call speech to cause trouble. But then again... It pained me to consider the possibility that she was actually telling the truth. If Susan was an imposter, what did that mean? Well, it meant that she was on the other side – whichever other side that was. This thought made me feel very uneasy indeed. If this really was the case, I had been very gullible. What else is new about that with me and women? On the other hand, if it was all a nasty lie... It was a dilemma. The thought chilled me to the marrow. But surely, I repeatedly tried to tell myself, it was just the case of the vicious old crone trying to stir up the waters. If Susan really was an imposter, she was a bloody good actress. I'd been in the front row of the stalls to witness how she reacted to the news of Frances' murder. There had been real tears and strong emotion. Still, that scenario was not impossible. Bluff, double bluff and triple bluff were the tricks of the nasty spy game. What was I to do? I grinned inwardly at this question. The answer was simple: I will do what I always do, what I have done with my life since I was in short trousers when presented with a problem that offered no easy answer. I would wait and see what happens while keeping my wits about me and my fingers crossed. I would, metaphorically, sleep with one eye open. And, of course, that was my only option.

The manager of Carter's Garage, the little outfit some two hundred yards up the road from the sweetie shop, was very obliging once he had seen the colour of my money. A bluff cocky bald-headed fellow in oil-stained overalls, he took great pride in informing me with a grim, arrogant smile that he was, in fact, *the* Mr Carter, the owner of the establishment. 'Been here since before the war. A respected business,' he'd crowed.

Apart from the money he extracted from my dwindling stash, he took as many details from me as he could, making a record of my identification card. I was surprised he didn't ask for my National Health number and my mother's dress size. My wallet was a great deal thinner as we drove away in a rather shabby Ford. I had it on loan for five days at an exorbitant rate and a veiled threat of something rather unpleasant happening to me if I did not return it on time and in excellent condition. 'We have ways of tracing "mislaid" vehicles,' I was told in a pointed manner.

Once we had completed the deal, we set off, navigating our way out of Rye. The route for Littlehampton was a straightforward one, passing through Maidstone.

'Why Littlehampton, do you think? What is there for him?' asked Susan as we left the environs of Rye.

'It's a small port with easy access to the English Channel. No doubt he hopes he'll be able to hire a boat to take him over to France or bribe some shady sailor to ferry him across.'

My main worry was whether we'd make it in time. Once in Littlehampton, we'd have to then start to search for the devil. That wasn't going to be easy, but one had to hope. Fingers crossed.

'What is your plan of action?' asked Susan as we hit the main road.

Not that one again. Well, if I had one, young lady, I wouldn't tell you, I thought to myself. Not just at the moment anyway. Not until I am sure whose side you are one. If you are the enemy, I'm sure you'll slip up and reveal yourself soon. Until then I'll keep my own counsel as much as I can. Apart from that – I haven't got a 'plan of action' anyway. It will be just a case of scouring the quayside looking for likely boats to hire or seeking out shady seafaring types and making enquiries. Slender indeed, but it was the best thing that I could come up with at the moment. But I kept that to myself.

'You'll see when we get to Littlehampton,' I said. It was a pathetic reply but it was the only one I could muster.

She obviously thought it sensible not to respond to this feeble statement and we both fell into silence.

We had gone about fifteen miles and were travelling on a fairly lonely track of road with rough flat moorland on both sides of us when I saw a figure at the side of the road ahead of us. It was a tall, burly man who seemed to be staggering as though drunk and waving his arms wildly at us, seemingly imploring us to stop.

I reduced speed but then the maniac suddenly stepped out into the middle of the road and placed himself was directly in our path. I slammed on the brakes and the tin can that was our motorcar squealed in agony at such effrontery, juddered violently in an irresponsible manner and swerved to the left before screeching to a halt just a few feet away from the man. He then stumbled forward and fell over the bonnet, his face glaring up us through the windscreen. Apart from his wild eyes and champing mouth, I noticed a savage cut to his forehead from which thick blood dribbled, leaving an ugly scarlet streak down his face.

Both Susan and I got out of the car and rushed to his assistance. Gently, we raised him off the car bonnet and led him on his shaky legs to the grass verge.

'He was a madman,' he muttered, the eyes still rolling erratically. 'A madman. This comes from being a Good Samaritan.' He gasped for air and tried to sit up.

Susan mopped his wound with a handkerchief.

'Take it easy. Rest for a moment,' I said.

'How can I rest after what happened?'

'What did happen? I asked, kneeling down by the man.

For the first time, his eyes focused on my face. 'He was a madman,' he said again. 'He attacked me. He... pulled out this gun – a real bloody gun, mind you. He ordered me to pull over. He said if I didn't he'd kill me.' He screwed up his eyes and his body shuddered with emotion. 'Bloody hell, it was a nightmare. Kill me! I ask you. Why would he want to kill me? I'd given the bastard a lift and that is what I get.'

I was tempted to ask questions at this juncture, but common sense told me to let the fellow get this awful experience out of his system first.

'I was slow to react to his threats so... the bastard hit me. He turned his gun on me and hit me with the butt, hit me hard. I saw stars, I can tell you. Stars and a bleeding thunder in my brain. He grabbed the wheel and tugged it, pulling into the side of the road. I tell you he was a bloody madman. How he got us to stop I don't know.'

At this point the poor devil froze, his eyes staring blindly into the sky. I thought for one moment he had stopped breathing and we had lost him. Susan and I exchanged concerned glances.

Then suddenly, he became animated again as though he had gained a second wind. 'Then he dragged me out of the cab and threw me on to the verge as though I was a sack of potatoes and then drove off with my lorry. With my lorry and its load. The bastard.'

'Who was he?' asked Susan.

'How the hell do I know?' came the furious response. 'He's a bloody madman, that's all I can tell you. A hitchhiker I had picked up out of the kindness of my heart and he does this to me.' Instinctively, his hand moved to his wound. 'And he's stolen my bloody lorry.'

It was obvious that his anger and frustration were anaesthetising his physical pain.

'Come along, I said, 'we'll get you to a hospital.'

'I don't need a bloody hospital. I need a police station to report this business: assault and theft.'

I nodded. 'OK. I reckon you'll live till you've done that but you certainly need that gash looking at. You might need stitches.'

'Nay, I'll be all right. I just want that bugger caught.'

'What did he look like?'

'He was just an ordinary bloke. In his thirties somewhere I should say – maybe tipping forty. He was in a blue suit but had no overcoat. I thought that strange. It's not that warm today. There was a bit of a frost this morning'. The man screwed up his eyes in an attempt to remember more. 'Fairly tall, clean-shaven – oh, and he had short blonde hair. Wore thin wirey-type glasses.' He gave a rough chuckle. 'I thought he was German until he spoke. He was English all right. The bastard!'

Susan and I exchanged looks. With that description, this had to be our Walter. In desperate need to escape and get to Littlehampton, he'd carried out this highway robbery. Surreptitiously, I placed a finger to my lips indicating to Susan not to say a word.

'Come on then, old chap, let's get you in our car and we'll get off to Maidstone and find you a cop shop.'

Without a word, he clambered stiffly into the back of the car. 'Thank you,' he said at last as I slipped into first gear and set off. 'I'm Herbert, by the way. Don't worry about me. I'll come round. I just want to report the attack to the police and hope they catch the scoundrel and get my lorry back. God knows what my boss will say about all this. I got a cargo of washing machines on board. Worth hundreds of pounds.'

I grinned at the irony of this. Walter and washing machines – united at last. 'Don't worry, Herbert. It will all be sorted out,' I said, trying hard to inject some conviction into my voice.

CHAPTER SEVENTEEN

Olga had pulled the car onto the verge two hundred yards behind the little grey Ford.

'What the hell is going on there?' asked Basil, Olga's companion, as they both stared out of the window and observed in the distance a man waving his hands in the air and staggering towards John Hawke's rented car.

'Is the fellow drunk or what?'

'It's "what", I suspect,' observed Olga dryly. 'In other words, a bloody complication, that's for certain.'

Basil groaned. He was remembering Sir Jeremy's anger at the lack of success in their endeavours and the threat that his words implied. And now here, in Olga's words, was another 'bloody complication.'

The pair stared in silence, mesmerised at the activities of Johnny and Susan and the staggering stranger, as though they were watching some strange silent film, a mixture of Max Sennett and Cecile B. DeMille. All that was missing was the tinkling piano accompaniment.

Once the stranger, who was obviously in some form of distress, had been helped into the back of the car it had set off once more, Olga revved up in readiness to follow.

'This is a bloody farrago,' muttered Basil to himself, rather than his companion, but Olga could not have agreed more.

CHAPTER EIGHTEEN
From the journal of Johnny Hawke

I had expected our new passenger to fall asleep once we were on the road again. The fellow had obviously had a savage blow to the head and the usual natural response to this was to escape into a comatose state to evade the pain and discomfort. But not old Herbert. Obviously, he was made of sterner stuff.

'He seemed a decent bloke when I picked him up,' he muttered, leaning forward from the back seat so that his face was very close to mine. 'Borrowed a map of mine and studied it hard at first.'

'Where did he say he was headed?' I asked.

'He was a bit vague about that. Somewhere near Littlehampton, I reckoned.' There was a pause and then: 'The bastard!'

'Once the police have details of your lorry, they'll soon be able to track him down, I'm sure.'

Suddenly, Herbert jerked forward and I found his hands gripping my shoulders. 'My God!' he cried. 'There it is. There's my lorry. Stop the car, stop the bloody car.' This outburst was screeched in my ear and his fingers dug harder into my shoulder. Instinctively, I obeyed his instruction and brought the car to a halt, although I had no idea what he was talking about.

'That roadside caff we just passed. My lorry… It was there. Parked outside. My bloody lorry.'

I stared into the rearview mirror and caught sight of the 'caff': Alf's Diner. I had been so focused on the road ahead that I'd passed it without my noticing. There were several cars parked outside and a couple of lorries.

'Are you sure?'

Herbert's voice went up a register. 'Of course I'm bloody sure. There it is, that green one – Bedford's Domestics. That's who I work for.'

'That must mean Walter's inside the café,' said Susan.

I nodded. 'Feeding his face without a care in the world.'

'Who is this Walter?' inquired Herbert.

'Never mind for the moment,' I said. 'Let's investigate.' I reversed the car up the road and pulled into the car park of Alf's Diner. In an instant, Herbert hopped out and ran to his lorry. He stroked it as though it was a precious pet.

'What now?' asked Susan.

'You and our chum stay outside – wait here while I go inside. If Walter is in there… well, I have a friend with me'. I patted my pocket which housed my revolver. 'I'd brought it with me on this excursion.

Susan frowned. 'Be careful, Johnny.' She seemed genuinely concerned, but then she may well have just been playing the part effectively.

'Just keep an eye on Herbert. We don't want any heroics from him. Keep him on a short rein.'

I made my way to the café. It was a low wooden structure, a little ramshackle in appearance, but gauging by the number of vehicles in the parking area, it seemed to be a thriving concern. I tried to peer in through the window but it was too steamed up to see clearly. There was nothing but to go inside.

Transport cafés situated on lonely stretches of road offer the tired driver a respite from the tedious task of getting from A to B without a break. They provide tea, simple grub, and that all-important lavatory. As a result, they usually do brisk business. Certainly, this one did. The place was heaving with customers. There were lorry drivers, a couple of families with youngsters in tow, and chaps in pinstriped suits all indulging in a mug of tea, buns, and various hot dishes. I noticed that the special of the day chalked on a blackboard near the counter was a spam fritter sandwich. I quite fancied one myself. It had been a long time since breakfast, but I was here for other reasons than my stomach.

Thankfully, my entrance did not generate much interest with the clientele. One or two turned their heads casually in my direction, almost as a reflex action to the door opening but they soon turned away again. As I made my way to the counter, I began scrutinising the faces of the diners. Although I had not seen Walter properly in his new persona, I assumed the short-cropped blonde hair would give him away, but as far as I could see, there was no one in the café with such a barnet. Maybe he had found a cap in Herbert's van and clapped that on his head. With this in mind, I scanned again. Still no joy.

'What can I get you?' asked the chap behind the counter, a middle-aged, rosy-cheeked fellow with a substantial stomach that was a fine advertisement for his spam fritters. I assumed this was the proprietor, Alf.

'Mug of tea…' Oh, well, I thought, what the heck. '… and the spam fritter sandwich.'

'Right you are, mate. Grab a table and I'll call out your order when it's ready.'

I nodded. This was ludicrous. I couldn't sit down and stuff spam fritters down my throat while Susan and Herbert were waiting outside. It was clear that Walter Clements wasn't dining here – well not now anyway. He must have abandoned the lorry and found himself another lift.

I was just about to head for the exit when out of the corner of my eye I saw the door of the gent's lavatory open – and who should emerge but my errant pal Wally Clements. There he was, blue suit, blonde hair, wire-rimmed glasses. It was him all right. He stood for a moment, his body tense as he surveyed the room. His eyes lit on me immediately. We had never met but it was clear that he knew me as well as I knew him. He sensed immediately that I was after him with that animal second sense that is instinctive to any desperate fugitive when coming into close proximity with their enemy. For a moment he froze and then, with a sudden jerky movement, he darted behind the serving counter and into the kitchen beyond.

'Hey! What the…' cried Alf in surprise. 'Come back here.'

His surprise increased when a second man slipped by him clumsily but at speed into the kitchen in pursuit of the intruder. That man was me.

The kitchen was manned by a young chap and an older woman who both became rigid with shock at this violent intrusion to their greasy frying world. Each stood, mouths agape, griddle pans in hand like domestic statues.

By the time I had crashed my way in, Walter had reached the

back door at the far end of the room. He glanced back and by heaven, the scoundrel has the gall to grin at me. The cheek of the bastard – he damned well grinned at me, as though we were playing a game. Then, yanking the key out of the lock, he passed through. I knew before I got there that he had locked the door. Well, that is what I would have done if the situation had been reversed. There was no point in trying to break the door down. Apart from the likelihood of doing myself an injury, it could take ages and no doubt Alf and others would have stopped me. There was only one sensible action to take and that was to turn, rush back through the kitchen and out of the café by the way I had entered, with the hope that I would catch old Walter as he rounded the corner of the building.

My immediate problem was proprietor Alf who was now bearing down on me with a look of thunder in his eyes and his bulky fists raised in pre-punch mode. Before he reached me, I pulled out my now ancient police warrant card and held it up before my face.

'Police!' I yelled with as much authority as I could muster. 'That man is dangerous. A fugitive from justice. I've got to get after him.'

The word 'police' and the seemingly official tatty warrant card magically halted Sam in his tracks.

'Surveillance operation,' I added, hoping to give greater gravitas and authenticity to my claim. 'Let me pass. I've got a man to catch.' Before Sam could respond, I squeezed past him and hastened through the kitchen into the body of the café. All eyes were on me as I made my way to the door, mesmerised by the dramatic shenanigans that were taking place, but thankfully, there were no would-be heroes who rushed forward in a dramatic attempt to stop me leaving.

Once out in the fresh air again, I gazed around, looking for my prey.

To my horror, surprise, amazement and a cocktail of other upsetting emotions, I spotted Clements ushering Susan into my car. It seemed to me that she was not offering any resistance. Slamming the passenger door, Walter rushed around to the driver's side and cast a swift glance towards the café where he spotted me. He grinned again and gave me a cheery wave with his hand, which held a gun. Within seconds he was in the driver's seat and revving the engine.

I raced forward but I knew it was a fruitless attempt to halt his getaway. With a roar and a cloud of dust, the car shot forward at speed out of the parking area, on to the road – and beyond my reach.

I swore loudly.

CHAPTER NINETEEN

'He certainly is a very tricky customer. He has dramatically upped his game since he's been on the run. Who would have guessed that tame little mouse – our errand boy at the Ministry – would turn into a cunning rat.' Olga smiled at her own imagery as she and Basil watched Walter slip into the driving seat of the grey Ford and speed away from the café car park.

'The chase continues,' she observed, as she pulled the Daimler off the grass verge back on to the road. As they drove on, she gave a brief chuckle as she saw John Hawke in the rear-view mirror emerging from the cloud of dust created by Clements' getaway. 'We're not the only ones he's fooled,' she said. 'Well, we're now on our own. Hawke is out of the picture. Now it's solely up to us to catch Clements. If we stick close to him, we should be able to nab him the next time he stops.'

Basil nodded. 'What I want to know is – why has he taken the girl? What does he want with her?'

Olga shrugged. 'A hostage or a bargaining tool if necessary. I don't know. Maybe he just acted on impulse.'

Basil pursed his lips. 'It just seems odd. Why should he burden himself in such a fashion at this stage of the game?'

'Well, it could work in our favour if it slows the bugger down.'

Olga was aware of the irony of this statement as soon as she had uttered it. Already the grey Ford was racing away from them. Instinctively, she pressed down on the accelerator. She was not going to lose Clements this time, whatever happened.

It did not take them long before they had caught up with the Ford. Olga kept her distance for a while, but she and Basil both knew what they had to do and when to do it. Basil was tracing the route on the map, his finger gently moving along the contours of the road.

'There's quite a long exposed stretch in about two miles. It seems there we are in the territory of fields on both sides again with no paved footpath,' he said.

Olga nodded with a wry smile. 'That sounds ideal. Should be fun'.

They drove on in silence for some ten minutes.

'Looks like this is the spot,' observed Basil as they ran into open terrain.

'Indeed. Time to speed up.' Olga pressed down on the accelerator

As luck would have it, there were no other vehicles on the road.

'I wonder if he's realised we are on his tail?' Basil pondered.

Olga just gave a gentle shrug in response. It really didn't matter now.

Olga increased her speed and pulled the car out to the right in preparation to overtake the Ford. Within seconds, the two cars were level. To Olga's delight, she observed Walter Clements turn his head in their direction, his face registering a mixture of shock and panic. It was obvious that he had recognised them. The Ford veered wildly for a moment as Walter attempted to retain control of the car and his emotions.

With a swift and firm turn of the wheel, Olga swung the car to the right causing it to collide with the Ford. There was a deafening clang and a scrape of metal, and both vehicles shook violently. The Daimler, being the sturdier car, had mastery of the situation and it forced the Ford sideways, causing it to edge closer to the verge and the ditch only feet away. Olga now pulled away and then pressed down on the accelerator until it hit the floor, causing the car to surge forward momentarily before she repeated the procedure of ramming the Daimler into the side of Clements' motor once more. Again, both vehicles shook violently on impact, but this time the force of the manoeuvre pushed the Ford even nearer the ditch, its outer wheels now running unevenly on the grass verge. Olga gave out a laugh of triumph as she gazed across to see Clements hunched over the wheel desperately trying to steer the shaking car away from the danger.

'No chance, comrade,' Olga muttered as she pulled away once more and then prepared to return and renew her assault. She was sure that one more prang would have him off the road and in the ditch. Meanwhile, Basil had wound down his window and was aiming a pistol at Clements. The Daimler closed in and he fired. There was a loud report and the side window of the Ford shattered but the bullet missed both the driver and the passenger. As the two vehicles collided once again with great force, Clements performed an unexpected manoeuvre. He braked hard, the Ford screeching to a juddering halt, slewing sideways, while the Daimler shot ahead down the road. Because of this shock tactic, Olga momentarily lost control and their car snaked across into the right-hand lane, rocking wildly, swerving in an erratic zig-zag fashion. In desperation, she wrestled with the wheel but the violent motion of the car caused her to press down harder on the accelerator pedal. The engine screamed and shot forward at greater speed, still on the wrong side of the road. This was not what she wanted to happen. It was as though her body had lost all sense of how to control the car. She froze as the speed increased.

'For God's sake, stop the bloody thing,' screamed Basil.

The words were received as just a noisy babble in Olga's ears, the ones sporting the bright dangling earrings. She stared ahead as though hypnotised by the ribbon of road which was flashing with great ferocity before her eyes.

Suddenly, from around a curve in the winding highway, there came the ominous shape of a petrol tanker. It was huge and shiny, speeding on a direct course towards them.

Olga screamed. She saw the inevitable before it happened. Her mind told her to wrench the steering wheel in order to pull the car back on to the left side of the road but her body was rigid with fear. In desperation, Basil reached over and grabbed the wheel, but it was too late. For a brief moment, time stood still for the two passengers in the doomed Daimler. They stared in horror at the bonnet of the oncoming tanker as it loomed up before them like a monstrous shadow. The car smashed with violent force headlong into the petrol tanker. Although the driver had braked when he saw the danger, it was not soon enough to prevent the inevitable. The tanker still roared forward, its tyres screeching and smoking in protest. The air was filled with the sound of grating and wrenching metal. As the front end of the Daimler concertinaed into the front of the tanker, the steering wheel was thrust violently against Olga's chest, crushing her ribs. The impact caused blood to fountain from her mouth and spill down her front. Meanwhile, Basil had been thrown forward with such strength, his head smashing through the windscreen, the jagged glass severing his jugular, a scarlet stream spurting copiously down the crazed glass. In the petrol tanker, the force of the collision had caused the driver to jerk forward, slamming his head on the dashboard. He slithered to the floor of the cab, unconscious.

And then the world exploded.

The force of the headlong crash had melded the two vehicles together, bonnet invading bonnet, with the result that both engines erupted in flames. In protest, the horn of the Daimler began blaring, as though in pain, as the conflagration grew in intensity and reached out towards the main body of the tanker and its lethal cargo.

The fire spread rapidly and very soon, there was simply one great wavering ball of yellow fire reaching up to the sky with only the vague outline of the two vehicles visible behind the fierce flickering curtain of yellow flame and dark suffocating, billowing smoke.

And then, as the fire found its way into the tanker shell there came an almighty roar as it erupted in a vivid yellow ball, the explosion sending shards of red hot metal high into the air. Within seconds, a giant black cloud hovered over the burning carnage below.

Watching this scene from some hundred yards away were Walter Clements and Susan Kershaw. After braking to a halt, Clements had reversed the car with the intention of doing a U-turn in the desperate hope of losing his pursuers. He was just about to carry out this manoeuvre when he saw the swaying Daimler racing directly into the path of the petrol tanker. He and Susan were held in grim fascination as the whole violent destructive scenario played out before them. It was all cataclysmic, unreal. Later, Clements likened it in his mind to the final dramatic scene in the James Cagney gangster movie

White Heat, where a gas storage tank explodes in tumultuous flames. 'Top of the world, ma!'

Both he and Susan were held mesmerised, staring in frozen amazement and horror as the two vehicles crashed and melded into each other. Soon, a ball of fire had engulfed both the car and the tanker.

Neither spoke to each other. The sight they had witnessed had temporarily robbed them of speech. They were both transfixed and hypnotised by the wavering flames and the dark billowing cloud. And then suddenly, Walter broke from his trance and slipped the car into first gear.

'What are going to do?' Susan asked, her voice a desperate and dry rasp.

'What the devil d'you think I'm doing? Getting the hell out of here.'

Before the car could gain momentum, Susan grabbed the door handle and yanked it down. The door slid open a foot.

'What do you think you're doing?' roared Clements.

'Getting out,' she cried and leapt from the vehicle, landing heavily on the grass verge.

'You bitch!' Clements cried, reaching out for her but failing to catch her arm. He let out a curse and brought the vehicle to a halt.

Susan was already on her feet and racing across the undulating grass terrain.

Walter jumped out and ran around the front of the car, which was now positioned almost parallel with the blazing carnage on the right-hand lane. As he moved, he could feel the heat of the flames on his face. Reaching into his coat pocket he retrieved his revolver and, aiming it at the fleeing figure, he fired. The crack of the pistol shot echoed across the grassland but it missed Susan by quite a distance. She was too far away for the range of the gun. A further expletive escaped his lips. Now he was unsure what to do. Should he follow her, try to capture her again or should he just make tracks as fast as he could? He hadn't time to debate this question for long – very soon other vehicles would arrive on this scene of fiery catastrophe and he could easily find himself being questioned and required as a witness. He certainly couldn't afford to tangle with the authorities. He gazed again across the grassy expanse. Susan was almost out of sight now, just a speck in the distance. He had to accept that he'd lost the girl. Bugger it! He would just have to forget her. He had his own skin to think about. Having her with him would have been useful but not essential. He cast a glance across at the blazing vehicles. At least he was rid of one lot of bastards on his tail – although he was in no doubt there would be others to replace them. Number One would see to that. Like the Hydra, you cut one head off and another grew in its place. And then, of course, there was that nuisance, the bastard with the eye patch. He knew little about him but in their brief encounter, he had got a full whiff of his dogged nature. Walter could see that the one-eyed terrier wasn't going to let this bone get away if he could help it

'Not out of the wood yet,' he muttered to himself as he returned to the Ford. In the distance, he could see two cars approaching. He needed to make himself very scarce. He jumped back into the driving seat and within seconds, he was speeding down the road, away from the flaming vehicles and that dark toxic cloud that loomed over them like some amorphous angel of death.

CHAPTER TWENTY
From the journal of Johnny Hawke

There are some moments in life when you wish the ground would open up beneath your feet and swallow you whole. As you slip down into the darkness, you are content in the belief that all the current problems and woes will be of no consequence in the subterranean void awaiting you. You will be free of all cares. It never happens, of course. One remains on terra firma, forced to face up to things. As I watched the little grey Ford containing Walter Clements and Susan Kershaw pull onto the main road out of the car park in a cloud of dust, along with my hopes of apprehending the devil, I wished for such a ground engulfing moment. No chance.

As I shook my head in despair, I was conscious of a figure approaching me. It was Herbert, who had emerged from a nearby clump of bushes where I assumed he had been hiding. His face was white with shock.

'What the hell…' I said, words almost failing me.

'He still had the gun. He threatened me with it again, the son of a bitch. He took the young lady with him.'

'I know. I saw that'.

'I couldn't stop him. He had the gun.'

'Yes. We have established that.' I saw that the drama was a simple one, and now dear Wally had a hostage… unless sweet Susan had gone willingly.

'Did he threaten the girl?' I asked.

Herbert shook his head. 'I don't know. I didn't see. I just ran for cover. What the hell do we do now?'

I took a moment to think. In truth, I was tired of thinking. My brain hurt. 'Well,' I said at length, 'we could try and follow in your lorry.'

As it happened, no we couldn't. There were no keys in the driving cab. Understandably. They were no doubt nestling in Walter's trouser pocket. I was tempted to swear again, but then my eyes lit upon something on the passenger seat that took all my attention. I snatched it up and examined it. What I held in my hands was an ordinance survey map of the south coast, but the most interesting thing about it were the detailed annotations. These, I assumed, had been made by Walter C, and they clearly indicated that his destination was not Littlehampton as I had first thought. An arrow drawn in pencil ran from Littlehampton further down the coast to a little place called Clovelly Bay. This was circled in pencil. No doubt this was intended to be Clements' jumping-off point for foreign shores. I could see the sense of this. Clovelly Bay would be a quieter place with a smaller community, less high profile than the busy fishing town of Littlehampton. It would probably be easier to hire a boat for a doubtful trip there.

So, now I knew for definite where to go. Well, sort of. What I didn't know was how I was going to get there.

'Is there any way we can get this crate of yours started without an ignition key?'

Herbert gave me a weary smile. 'No, not at all, but we don't have to worry about that. We'll just use a key.'

'You may have noticed, but there isn't one,' I snapped back.

'Yes, there is. My spare. I'd be a poor sort of a delivery driver if I didn't have a spare.' He leaned forward and reached under the shelf on the passenger's side, pulled back a strip of black tape and produced a shiny ignition key. 'I keep this here in case of emergencies,' he said with a grin.

I could not help but join him in the smile. 'Well, what are we waiting for, let's get off.'

I had no delusion that we would catch up with Walter Clements – he was in a much faster vehicle than this chugging old lorry laden with washing machines, but at least we were on his tail. When we reached Maidstone, I hoped that I could pick up another hire car to speed off to Clovelly Bay.

Once we were one the road again, Herbert turned to me. 'What is this business all about? You some sort of copper?'

'Yes, some sort of copper. A private one.'

'And who is this geezer you're after – the one that biffed me with his gun?'

'To be honest, I'm not sure. He may be a murderer. He may

be a spy.' I bit my tongue as soon as I'd said that. What a stupid oaf.

'A spy!' The voice went contralto.

'Not really,' I said as casually as I could, 'I was just joshing. Just a low life ne'er do well, that's all.' I grinned a grin that would fool no one.

'Come on mate,' said Herbert leaning closer. 'Tell me all about it.'

'The less you know, the better, Herbert. Just let's get to Maidstone, you can drop me off there and then forget all about what's happened in the last few hours and get on with the rest of your life.'

'You said spy? You mean one of those Ruskie bastards? I read about them all the time in the papers.'

'Don't worry your head about it. It's not a matter of national security, just a minor problem.' Here I go, lying again. I did know that it was a matter of national security and not a little transgression like an out of date fishing licence. But I was not about to spill the beans to my new friend, the washing machine delivery driver. Who knows who he would go blabbing to if I did? All this espionage stuff was alien to me, but there was murder involved – and that certainly was my territory. Whatever the nature of the tangled web I was enmeshed in, I knew it was best to keep my lip firmly buttoned.

Thankfully, Herbert accepted my explanation and lapsed into silence. We chugged along nicely for a while when suddenly, his body stiffened and he gave a little cry of alarm. 'Hello, what's going on here?' he growled.

His right hand flew from the steering wheel and pointed to the road ahead. I followed the aim of his outstretched arm and saw several vehicles, including a police car and a fire engine, assembled at the roadside by a tangled burning wreck of metal, the result of some terrible accident. As Herbert slowed down, I could see that there was a car and a large lorry which appeared to have crashed into each other. All that was left of them were their mangled skeletal frames faintly visible through the flickering sheet of fire that engulfed them. As I leaned further forward to gain a better view, I was able to observe through the smoke and flames the blistered number plate at the rear end of the car. To my great surprise, I realised that I had seen it before. It was the one that I had noted when I'd been shot at outside the Clements' house. The car I had been seeking at Parkinson's garage. Surely this was no coincidence. How did it get here? What on earth had happened? What kind of bizarre scenario did it suggest? My mind began spinning again as I tried to work out what this all meant. That number plate clearly indicated that it was the enemy's car. How had they ended up in this part of the world? Well, I reckoned the answer to that question must be the obvious one. They had either followed me or Walter C. For whatever reason, their pursuit had ended in disaster. Did they know where he was going or, like me, were they just feeling their way in the dark? Well, one thing was for sure, they would not be feeling their way anymore. It was clear no one could have survived that crash.

'Rather nasty,' observed Herbert dryly.

'Move on,' I said.

'With pleasure,' replied Herbert with grim enthusiasm.

Herbert revved up the lorry and we drove past the smoking carnage.

We continued our journey, my mind still whirling with muddled thoughts and wondering how this rather dark and dangerous episode that I'd got myself wrapped up in would end.

CHAPTER TWENTY ONE

From the safety of a small copse not far from the highway, the woman calling herself Susan Kershaw had witnessed the crash and the resulting conflagration. With the arrival of the police and the fire engine, she had been prepared to break cover and announce herself as a witness, hoping that the police would take her back to civilisation. The fake documents in her purse should secure safe passage, probably to Maidstone. These papers would ensure that no difficult questions would be asked and that she would not be detained for questioning. She needed to get in touch with Sir Jeremy and bring him up to date on the case.

Just as she was about to leave the wooded area, she saw Herbert's lorry approaching along the road. She was held for a moment. Tempting as it was to rush forward and flag it down, she did not want to encounter John Hawke again. Things had become too complicated. He would only hinder her now. His mission to find Clements was different from hers and she was also fairly sure that he had grown slightly suspicious as to her motives. Her story had hung together nicely to begin with, but she had sensed that it had now begun to unravel. Hawke was no fool and it was only a matter of time before he sussed out the truth, and that would put her in danger. It was, therefore, prudent to steer clear of him – for the time being, at least. Association with Hawke would only hinder her efforts. He had proved useful for a time but now she needed to act alone.

She waited until the lorry had passed by before leaving the shelter of the copse and making her way to the roadside and towards the police car.

Walter Clements drove on like an automaton, his mind deep in thought. He was trying to sort out his life; the past, the present and, more importantly, the future. *Yes*, he admitted to himself, *I suppose I am a spy*. It was the first time he had really considered himself as such. He had previously thought that he was just a petty thief: purloining bits of information for ready cash. On the other hand, in doing so, he had achieved a kind of status within the organisation of his new masters – a status that he had never achieved in any other area of his life before. For the first time in his life, he had become someone of consequence. He was important to them. But that was in the past. Now they wanted rid of him. And the British authorities would be after him, too, so now, yes, he had to accept that he was a spy. However, he was not one of those trained individuals who know how to fight and kill and perform adventurous, energetic escapades. He was just an office waller who had been in the right place for the Russians to be interested in him and offer him substantial remuneration for obtaining certain information. Indeed, it was the money, rather than any political leanings that secured his cooperation. In his naiveté, he saw no real danger in his actions. It was just a matter of simple subterfuge. The fact that his life had gradually become built on lies did not matter to him. In fact, it added spice to his otherwise dull existence – dull, that is, until the last few days when his world had been turned upside down. He wasn't naturally a brute and a bully, but it seemed that he had become one. And he had never handled a gun before – not even in the war – but now he had been on the verge of using it, of shooting someone. Well, he may still have to do that to preserve his freedom. He had become a desperate man, and desperate men take desperate measures.

However, one thing was paramount now: he had to escape. They hang traitors in this country and just silence them in Russia. Either way, if he got caught, he was dead meat. So, no matter how much he would like to pull into the side of the road and take a refreshing nap, he knew he could not afford to waste the time. One lot of pursuers had been eliminated – through their own carelessness – but who knows how many more were on his trail? He must press on.

Ahead, there was a road sign which quickened his pulse: Maidstone 5 Miles. Once he had passed this town, his goal was in sight. However, he was also conscious that he was driving a stolen vehicle and it was likely that the police would be on the lookout for it. He decided that he had best ditch the car in Maidstone and acquire another for the last leg of his journey.

He gave a long weary sigh. How the hell was all this going to end?

David Llewellyn was just about to leave his office when the telephone rang. He groaned. He had planned to get off early today. He had a birthday party to go to. His daughter's. He hoped the call wasn't an important having-to-stay-behind-and-sort-it-out business. He had missed Belinda's last two birthday shindigs because of work and he had promised her most faithfully that he would be there to watch her blow out the nine candles on the cake.

'Yes?' he said, his tone brusque and weary.

'You seem a cheerful chappie,' said the voice at the other end.

'Johnny?'

'Yes, just.'

'Where are you?'

'I'm in Maidstone.'

David raised his eyebrows in surprise. 'What the heck are you doing here?'

'On the trail of our traitorous friend, Walter.'

David sat back down at his desk, leaning forward to rest the arm holding the receiver. 'Tell me all.'

Johnny did as he was asked. He prided himself in being well able to self-edit accounts of his exploits to include only the salient points. David made notes during the concise recital.

'Where d'you reckon the girl fits into this jigsaw?' asked David, now starting to doodle on his note pad.

'I'm not sure. I don't know if she went willingly with Clements or he forced her. It seems strange that he'd want to burden himself with her when he was desperate to make a quick getaway – and I can't forget what the old woman said about Mrs Clements never having a sister. Can you check up on that?'

'Certainly. What are your plans now?'

'Grab another car and head for Clovelly Bay. The place is small enough for me suss out something. He'll be on the lookout for a small boat holder who is prepared to take him across the channel. Keep your fingers crossed I can catch up with him before he sets sail.'

'Good luck, boyo. I'm afraid I'll have to leave the matter to you. If I get the police involved down in the Maidstone area, I'll have the bully boy from National Security kicking my arse. I'm not supposed to be involved, remember.'

'I remember.'

'So for the moment, I'm afraid you're on your own.'

'What else is new?'

'I just wish you good luck. Once we can grab Clements for certain then I can mobilise my forces. Keep me up to date as and when you can. Ring me here or at home. I've got to be there soon. It's Belinda's birthday and we are having a party, I can't afford to miss it.'

A children's party, thought Johnny. *How normal, how wonderfully ordinary.* For a fleeting moment, he wished he could be involved that every day domestic world, away from gun-toting renegade spies and dead bodies. He could blow up balloons and organise games of blind man's buff and musical chairs. With a shrug of the shoulders, he erased such foolish thoughts from his mind.

'Little Bel,' he said cheerfully. 'Gosh, how old is the little scamp now?'

'She's nine.'

'That makes me feel old.'

'How do you think it makes daddy feel?'

'Do you think we're too ancient to be doing what we keep on doing? Chasing desperate fellows in an attempt to bring them to justice.'

There was a pause on the line before David responded. 'Probably, boyo, but I reckoned we're programmed to do it and there's no way we can switch off. It's in our blood. It's what we do.'

'It's what we do,' Johnny repeated softly. 'Have a happy party. Give Bel a kiss from me. Cheers for now.' Then the line went dead.

CHAPTER TWENTY TWO
From the journal of Johnny Hawke

Dowson's Motors looked rather a down at heel establishment located in a dingy street not far from the centre of Maidstone. It had been recommended by the taxi driver I had commandeered after bidding Herbert a fond farewell and ringing David with the latest news. Herbert had been quite sweet in his goodbyes. 'Nice to have met you, Johnny,' he said, his tired face wrinkling into a grin. 'It's been a bit of fun ain't it. Certainly brought a bit of excitement into my mundane old life.'

I shared his grin. 'Don't knock the mundane. It's nice and safe, and it's not life-threatening. I could do with a bit of mundane myself just now.'

'Ah, whatever. I wish you well. Now I'd better be on my way, I've this load of washing machines to deliver and I am somewhat late due to unforeseen circumstances.'

We shook hands and I clambered out of the cab as he revved up his engine. I waved him off and strangely, I was a little sad to see him go. Now I really was on my own.

As I stood on the forecourt staring up at the sign of Dowson's garage, a ferret faced man in a tired pin-striped suit materialised by my side. I assumed that he had emerged from the darkness of the cavernous interior of the garage workshop, where I had glimpsed the ghostly outlines of several motor cars.

'Can I help you squire?' he said smoothly, his lips hardly moving.

'I need to hire a car.' (*The second time today*, I thought, *but I wouldn't want to tell you what happened to the first one!*)

He rubbed his hands together enthusiastically. 'Well, you've come to the right place. Have you any kind of chugger in mind?'

I shook my head. 'Just something that will get me from A to B quickly.'

'And how long d'you want it for?'

I had to think about this. God, I hope I could wrap this business up swiftly. 'Two days, I guess.'

The man turned from me and moved towards the dark workshop and called out. 'Terry! Come here, sunshine, we got a customer.'

There was a muffled response from inside and within seconds, a tousled haired youth in blue overalls appeared, carrying a spanner in his left hand.

'Terry, this gent is after hiring a car. He's wanting a nippy little beggar. I thought the Morris Oxford. Could you bring it round to the front?'

Terry grinned. 'No can do. It went out a couple of hours ago.'

'I never saw it go.'

'It was when you were at the pub... having lunch. I marked it down in the book. The money's in the till.'

'A Morris Oxford, you say,' I said, addressing the youth, a small alarm bell ringing in my head.

'Yeah, nice little motor.'

'Was it a man who hired it?'

Terry nodded.

'Can you describe him?'

Terry frowned. The sudden change in conversation had obviously puzzled him.

'What?' he said.

'Can you tell me what he looked like?'

Terry shrugged. 'Just normal, I guess.'

'Did he have a moustache?'

He thought for a moment. 'I don't think so.'

'What about his hair?' What colour was his hair?'

'It was fair.'

'Short cropped, blonde?'

'Yeah, yeah, I reckon so.'

'And he wore steel-rimmed glasses?'

Terry nodded.

It had to be him. I would have bet my last half-crown that this was Walter.

'And he took the Morris Oxford, you say?'

I could tell from the mixed expression on Terry's face, one of puzzlement and a touch of irritation, that he was uneasy with this questioning.

'Are you wanting a vehicle or not?' intervened the pin-striped cove.

'Oh, yes, of course. What have you got?'

'Terry, what's left?'

'There's always the Triumph Roadster – she's a nifty beast.'

'A top-class motor. Certainly for speed, she's your best bet – but she comes at a premium price. It's a further quid a day extra,' muttered Mr Pin Stripe.

I ignored the ridiculously exorbitant charge. I had no choice in the matter. 'Fine. I'll take it.'

Now there were smiles all round.

'Right squire, if you'll just come into the office to sign the papers and settle the payment, Terry will bring the motor round to the front for you.'

I nodded and Terry gave a casual salute to his boss and disappeared into the gloom of the garage. I followed Mr Pin Stripe into his cramped little office, which smelt of petrol and damp. As he began to sort out the paperwork, I leaned on his desk in a nonchalant fashion. 'Would you mind,' I said casually, 'letting me have the details of colour and number plate of that Morris Oxford which went out earlier?'

'That again,' my companion frowned. 'What is all this?'

I could see that I wasn't going to get the information I needed unless I provided an explanation – a reason for my interest in the car. I wasn't about to reveal the truth so I'd have to come up with some kind of realistic, believable fairy tale. I gave a cheeky grin and launched forth.

'I suppose I'd better come clean,' I said, expanding the grin into a beaming smile. 'I'm in a race with a chum. We have a bet on to see who can get to Rye first using hired vehicles and I think he's the chap who rented the Morris Oxford from you. Short blonde hair, glasses, well built. Be too much of a coincidence if it was anyone else.' (That part of the lie was true). 'I'd just like to know if he's the chap who took your car so I can keep a lookout for him.'

It was a feeble tale but told in such a jaunty fashion that it seemed as though I had convinced Mr Pin Stripe.

'How much is on the bet?'

'A crisp twenty.'

For a moment Mr Pinstripe stared at me, his face blank, without any recognisable expression and then suddenly he grinned. 'Well,' he said, 'I reckon you'll be saying goodbye to your crisp twenty. Your mate has got at least a good two hours start on you and that Morris is very nippy little motor.'

I nodded glumly. 'I know the odds are against me, but I've got to press on'.

He did not reply but picked up a ledger from his desk and flipped it open. 'Is your mate's name Martin, James Martin?'

For a moment, I was in a quandary. It struck me that Walter C would not give his real name and then again this James Martin may very well be a real person. Of course I realised I just had to say yes.

'Yes, that's him,' I said.

'Yeah, he took the Morris. AC234. It's dark green.'

'Thank you.' I said, making a mental note of the number.

'Now, I reckon we'd better conclude our little transaction so you can be on your way and hope your pal calls for a pint somewhere and gives you a chance to catch up with him.'

'Yes, indeed,' I replied with enthusiasm.

Within ten minutes I was speeding out of Maidstone. I had tried contacting David to give him details of the car, but he wasn't at the office and I knew I couldn't pass on the information to anyone else at the Yard because my old chum was not supposed to be involved in the case. He could arrange for the police to look out for the car and, if it was spotted, have it stopped and the driver detained on some trumped up charge. Failing to get through to David at the Yard, I rang him at home and the phone was answered by a child who was fairly inarticulate. In the background, I could hear the screeching of youngsters. Of course. It was Bel's birthday party. After a few garbled mutterings from the child she put the phone down. I gave up and jumped back into the car. I guess I was being left to my own devices for the time being. I put my foot down and within the hour was passing through Littlehampton. Shortly afterwards, I passed the signpost that informed me that Clovelly Bay was about thirty-five miles away. It was a small place and so the haystack would be smaller, but I still had to locate that needle.

CHAPTER TWENTY THREE

Walter Clements was weary. His whole body craved a rest. It had been a most stressful two days and all he wanted to do was sleep – escape into the darkness of slumber. The thought of sinking down on a soft mattress, his head lying on a downy pillow and crisp white sheets up to his chin and closing his eyes on the world was all he really wanted to do. It was a foolish notion but he hoped that, in Shakespeare's words, sleep would knit up his own very ravelled sleeve of care. But deep down, he knew the only thing that would aid his pain was flight – safe flight. To escape the boundaries of England and those pursuers who were determined to destroy him. So, as his eyes hooded with tiredness, he bit his lip to keep himself alert and focused on the road. A sign for Clovelly Bay quickened his spirit.

Sir Jeremy was just pouring himself the first sherry of the evening when Barnes, his manservant, entered after a discreet knock.

'Sorry to bother you, sir, but there is a call on the red phone.'

Sir Jeremy raised a fluffy grey eyebrow. 'Who is it?'

'Elsa, sir.'

Sir Jeremy placed his sherry glass down on the drinks tray and, with a brief nod of acknowledgement to Barnes, he hurried to his office, closing the door behind him.

'S.J. here,' he intoned, picking up the receiver. 'I am still puzzling about the number.'

'It is 30.'

'And the month?'

'September.'

He gave a sigh 'Elsa, my dear it is so good to hear your voice. Are you safe and well?'

'Yes, I'm fine.'

'That is a relief. So then to business. Regarding the Clements matter, what news from the Rialto?'

'I am in Maidenhead en route for Clovelly Bay, along the

south coast from Littlehampton which is where our subject is headed. He inadvertently let slip his final destination when I was his passenger.'

'His passenger? What on earth do you mean?'

'Quite a lot has happened today'

'Tell me.'

'I will be brief.'

'Always wise, but make sure all relevant points are covered.'

'Of course.'

'Good girl.'

The woman who had called herself Susan Kershaw relayed all her adventures that day since setting off with Johnny Hawke for Rye. As she did so, Sir Jeremy made a few notes in the jotter on his desk.

When she finished her recital, there was a brief pause before Sir Jeremy responded. 'Unfortunately, we have no agents in that neck of the woods whom I can contact, so the whole business is down to you, I'm afraid.'

'I thought that would be the case. Don't worry, I am sure I can handle the matter.'

Sir Jeremy smiled. 'I am sure you can, but please, my dear, take all precautions necessary. You know, of course, that it is imperative that we get hold of Clements and without any involvement with this Hawke fellow. He must be kept in the dark about the reason we're after our man. Hawke is a tricky fellow and could cause us serious problems, and that would never do.'

'I appreciate that, but he is a decent man ...'

'That may be so, but he is a civilian and works for our enemies and, as such, is a potential threat to the secret nature of our organisation. If it comes to it, he may well have to be eliminated.'

After the telephone conversation, Susan stood for some time in the airless telephone box while she tried to come to terms with her burden of responsibility. At no point had she contemplated the notion that she may well have to get rid of Johnny Hawke. To silence him. Her training had equipped her to subjugate emotions while on a mission. There was no room for feelings in her line of work. However, she had never had to deal with the situation of eliminating someone she had got to know, someone she liked and believed to be, as she had told Sir Jeremy, 'a decent man.' She had not really considered him 'the enemy', but now she had to face the fact that he was. In essence, he worked for the other side and he had to be regarded as expendable. She just hoped that it would not come to that particular crunch. With a deep sigh, she pushed open the heavy door of the telephone box and breathed in the cool fresh evening air. At the moment, her main concern was how to get to Clovelly Bay and then locate Walter Clements.

The sun was setting, sending long fingers of amber light along the pavement. It was just after six o'clock and all the shops were closed for the day, blinds drawn, doors shut and the streets eerily empty. She had to get to Clovelly but it was too late to try and hire a car… so there was only one other alternative. As she turned the corner of the road into a narrow alley which ran behind a row of terraced houses, the answer to her dilemma presented itself. There, leaning against a tall wooden gate, was a motorbike. It was an Ariel Red Hunter. Thanks to her training, she knew about motorbikes. It wasn't a new model, at least five years old, but it had obviously been well looked after and appeared to be in good condition. The red paintwork gleamed as did the silver spokes. The bike was chained to a hook in the wall – a hook that did not look too secure.

Checking that there was no one about on the alley, she began to tug at the chain. Initially, a small shower of dust spluttered forth and the hook appeared to loosen a little but then as she renewed her efforts, pulling as hard as she could, the fastening held firm. Taking her purse from her jacket pocket, she extracted a nail file and began scraping away at the wall by the base of the hook. Eventually, after much prodding, the brickwork began to crumble away. She carried on for another few minutes and then tried tugging at the hook again. This time it shifted, allowing her to afford herself a grim smile. Another bout of scraping with the nail file and finally the hook surrendered and she was able to yank it from the wall, thus freeing the bike.

Returning the file to her purse and extracting a thick piece of wire, she set about tackling the ignition. It was another skill she had developed during her training. Manipulating the wire with her nimble fingers soon brought the engine to life.

Within seconds, she was astride the bike and riding away down the alley.

CHAPTER TWENTY FOUR

Clovelly Bay was a tiny fishing village which, in some respects, time had passed by. There had been no new building there in over a hundred years. With its ancient cobbled streets and simple cottages huddled by the meandering seafront, any character from a Victorian novel would feel at home here. Apart from the hardy fisherfolk, there were very few other inhabitants. There was no school, no police station and just one small general store. Young people either carried on the family tradition of fishing or left as soon as they were able to seek their fortunes and a better life elsewhere.

Clovelly was in a dip on the coast road and approached and exited by two steep hills. As he drew near to the village, Walter Clements pulled the car into the side of the road halfway down the hill. It was dusk, and below him he could see the twinkling lights of the village, a myriad of pinpricks in the growing gloom, like earthly stars. He decided to walk the rest of the way, thinking that a car stopping in the village would cause a certain amount interest and curiosity. That was the last thing he wanted.

Turning his collar up against the evening chill, he made his way down to the seafront. The place seemed deserted. All was quiet apart from the gentle lapping of the waves against the quay. Here was an array of fishing boats in a variety of sizes, silent silhouettes bobbing up and down as though they were excited to see him. He walked along the length of the quay, looking for a boat that would suit him – one that could take him to France. He knew that he hadn't the skill to tackle the trip on his own. Stealing a boat, even if he could manage it, was out of the question. He lacked any experience of sailing or nautical map reading. He had no intention of leaving his pursuers behind just to end up in Davy Jones' Locker. No, he would need someone to take control of the navigation and all that seafaring stuff. Someone he could bribe to take him across the water.

As he studied the range of vessels carefully, he was aware that he had to find one that wasn't too big. He needed a boat that could be handled by one man. A larger crew would be too risky. There were a few likely candidates who could fit the bill, but one in particular took Clements' fancy. It was a trim one-masted trawler-type boat called Aurora. Checking that there was no one lurking in the darkness on the deck, he stepped aboard the boat. It seemed sturdy and compact enough for his purpose. Peering through a porthole, he observed that there was even a small cabin with a bunk bed.

Satisfied that he had found the boat to suit his needs, he returned to the quay and made his way to the local pub, The Crown and Anchor, which he had observed as he entered the village. A pub was the place in which to find things out – and he needed to discover who owned the Aurora. He hoped that this fellow could be persuaded with a bunch of white fivers.

As he entered the smoky, dimly lighted inn, all eyes of the inhabitants turned in his direction. The room was full of fishermen who eyed this intruder into their domain with dark curiosity. Strangers were regarded not just with suspicion, but with a certain amount of animosity in this neck of the woods. The locals were used to the odd tourist taking a lunchtime pint before moving on, but a stranger was a rarity in the evening and someone to be wary of. No one came to Clovelly after dark.

Clements gave a gentle smile and nodded his head agreeably to the assembled throng as though meeting a set of old friends. It was a futile gesture. His pleasantry was not reciprocated. Slowly the men turned back to their pints and hushed conversations. He quickly made his way to the bar.

The barman did not speak but raised a quizzical eyebrow in anticipation.

'A pint of bitter.'

He was served in silence.

Clements handed over a shilling and waited for his change which was dropped on the counter in a puddle of beer.

'Thank you,' he said smiling at the taciturn barman. 'I wonder if you could help me.'

The barman gave a dry grin which revealed a row of stained uneven teeth. 'I doubt that very much,' he said.

'It's about a boat. One down by the quayside. The Aurora.'

'Oh, yes?'

'I wondered if you knew who owned it.'

'What's it to you?'

'I was wondering if it was for hire?'

The barman pursed his lips.

'You have money?'

'Yes, I have money,' Clements replied, quickly realising that this may be a dangerous confession to make. He gazed across the room at all the beady eyes fixed upon him.

'You could have a word with Sam Brewer about it,' said the barman.

'Where can I find him?'

The barman leaned forward, his lips forming into a cold unpleasant grin. 'Well... I could tell you but round here information don't come cheap.'

What Clements wanted to do was slosh his pint into the fellow's mug, followed by a quick punch to the nose. That's what he wanted to do, but instead, he reached his hand into his jacket pocket. 'How much?' he asked.

The barman's eyes glinted with greedy pleasure. 'I reckon a fiver might do the trick.'

'A fiver!'

'As I said, information don't come cheap 'round here. Please yourself, squire.'

He was about to move away but Clements stretched out his hand and touched the barman's arm. 'Wait,' he said.

'Take your hand off me, feller.' There was snarling violence in this riposte.

'A fiver, you say,' said Clements, retrieving his wallet from his jacket.

'A fiver, I say.'

Clements extracted a five-pound note and passed it over to the barman who quickly stowed it away in his back pocket.

'Now where can I find this Sam Brewer?'

The barman was positively beaming now and even allowed himself a little chuckle. 'You see that fat old bloke with the Father Christmas beard in the corner...' he said nodding his head in that direction.

'Yes. Is that him?'

The barman chuckled again. He was enjoying his little game. 'No that ain't him.'

'What are you playing at here? You've got your money...'

'Easy boy,' came the reply. 'The thin rat-faced bloke who's talking to Santa Claus. Well, that's Sam Brewer. He was right under your nose all the time.' Now he laughed out loud before turning away and patting his back pocket.

Once again, Clements wanted to thump the bastard on the nose and wipe the satisfied expression off his face, but instead, he allowed himself a whispered expletive, picked up his pint glass and moved over to where Sam Brewer was seated. As he approached the table, the old man with the white beard began roaring with laughter as though he had just been fed the punch line of a dirty joke.

Clements waited for the laughter to subside before he spoke. 'Excuse me, Mr Brewer...'

The thin-faced fellow stared up at him with mean weasel eyes. 'Who wants to know?' he snarled.

'I wonder if I could have a private word with you?'

'What about?'

'It's a matter of business.'

'Business, eh? Well, it is very kind of you to buy me a pint along with a whisky chaser.' He raised his eyebrows in anticipation.

'Certainly,' said Clements.

Brewer turned swiftly to the old man. 'Make yourself scarce, Chalky, I gotta talk to this geezer on a matter of business... after he's got the drinks in.'

Without a word, the old man heaved himself out of his chair and wandered off.

'Now then,' said Brewer, 'those drinks...'

Clements bought the drinks and returned to the table.

Brewer downed half of the pint of beer before he spoke, white froth still clinging to his lips. 'So, what is the nature of this business you want to talk about?'

'You are the owner of the Aurora.'

Brewer pursed his lips. 'What if I am?'

'I'd like to hire it.'

Brewer grinned. 'I'm sorry, matey, I no longer do trips around the bay.'

'I want you to take me to France.'

The grin disappeared. 'Come again?'

'I want… need to get to France. Can you get me over there? I can pay you well.'

Brewer said nothing for a while before leaning forward across the table. 'For that, you'll have to pay me very well indeed. What you're asking is illegal.'

'I know but I've just got to get across the channel.'

'You been a bad lad then?'

'That doesn't matter. Will you do it?'

Again, Brewer did not reply immediately as his brow puckered in thought. It took a while before he replied. 'It will cost you, matey.'

'How much?'

'I reckon the trip's worth a hundred quid,' he replied glibly before downing the rest of his pint.

Clements knew he couldn't argue or bargain. It would diminish his stash of cash, but he had to accept the offer. 'OK,' he said. 'Fifty quid when we set sail and the other fifty when we get there'.

Brewer considered this arrangement for a moment, his lips moving as though he was chewing a tough piece of beef. 'OK, matey. I reckon I can live with that, but I'll need to see the colour of your money first. I'm not preparing to set off for this voyage without being certain that you can cough up with the readies, if you catch my drift.'

Clements caught his drift and surreptitiously opened his wallet to reveal a thick wad of white notes. Brewer's eyes bulged at the sight.

'Oh, you have been a bad lad ain't you? Must have to be so desperate.'

Clements ignored this comment. 'When can we get going?' he asked, stowing his wallet away.

'Hang on a minute, matey. This isn't a pleasure boat trip in an amusement park, you know. I'll need to make some preparations and bring over sufficient fuel from my lock up to make sure I get there and back. That's going to take me an hour or so.' He checked his watch. 'It's just after eight now. There is a shelter on the quay about two hundred yards from where the Aurora's berthed. I'll meet you there at ten on the dot. Is that a deal?'

Clements nodded. 'It's a deal.'

'And no funny business'.

'I've finished with funny business. I just want to get away.'

'OK matey, give me fifty now and don't forget to bring the rest of the cash with you.'

Clements counted out the notes and passed them over. Brewer clawed them into his back pocket before raising the whisky glass as though in a toast before gulping it down.

CHAPTER TWENTY FIVE
From the journal of Johnny Hawke

As my flickering headlights picked out the road sign that told me I was only one mile from Clovelly Bay, I heaved a sigh of relief. The end was in sight. Or so I hoped. I had no idea what kind of end that would be – no doubt some surprising dark cornucopia of events, but I had waded so deep in these treacherous waters that I had to carry on and hope for the best. The problem was that after a somewhat eventful day my mind and body were tired and ragged.

I gazed ahead of me. Surely, somewhere down in that little seaside fishing hamlet was Walter Clements desperately seeking a way to escape to France. He may have already made it. If so, my job was done; my mission a failure. I couldn't hire a canoe and paddle after him. But, if he was still lurking by the waterfront, I hoped I could grab him. He was a traitor after all. He had not murdered anyone as far as I could tell – others were responsible for the death of my client, his wife who had employed me to find him. Of course, he had stolen secrets to pass on to the Ruskies and that made him a very naughty boy. And as far as I knew, he was still in possession of the microfilm. It was vital that it was retrieved before it fell into the hands of the Russians.

As I drove down the hill towards the village, I observed a car at the side of the road. It was a Morris Oxford with the number plate old Pin Stripe Charlie had given me. The car was parked awkwardly. It was obviously Clements' motor. I pulled in and investigated but, as I suspected, there was no one in the car. Running my hand across the hood, it was cool to the touch, which told me that the car had been here for some time. However, now I knew that Master Clements could not be far away. In a methodical fashion, I visited each tyre and let it down until it was flat as the proverbial pancake. No way was my mate Clements going use this as a getaway vehicle.

Satisfied with my handiwork, I returned to my car and

continued down the hill. I parked at the edge of the village and
made my way to the seafront. It was a clear, cool evening with
a bright full coin of a moon beaming in a cloudless sky. There
was no one about and an eerie blanket of silence seem to lie
softly on the sleepy hamlet. There was an array of fishing
vessels tied up along the quay, dark silhouettes gently shifting
in the water. My heart sank as I made my way along the
quayside. If Walter Clements was about he was making a good
job of it, hiding in the shadows. There was no sign of any
activity on any of the vessels in view. If he had hired a boat, it
probably had already sailed.

Eventually, I came to the end of the row of boats so that there
was nothing between me and the sea, the black undulating
waters streaked with silver slivers of moonlight. I stood on the
edge of the quay and stared out into the distance. Was Mr C out
there, bobbing up and down on the channel, heading for
freedom and obscurity? With a kind of gentle cruel irony, the
expression of 'having missed the boat' came to my mind. I
heaved a heavy sigh and was just about to retrace my steps when
I saw something, a dark shape, floating on the water, rising and
falling, tugged hither and thither by the undulating tide. I leaned
forward and stared. Was I seeing things or was that…? By Jove,
I wasn't wrong: it was… it was a body.

It was face down in the water with its arms flung wide like
wings. The top half was floating on the surface, but the lower
portion was below the waterline. I was able to determine that it
was a man and I could also see that he had light coloured hair –
probably blonde. My goodness – was it Clements? How could
that be? Had the desperate bastard committed suicide, throwing
himself into the cold unforgiving waters? Was he dead? Well,
it looked like it, but one could not be certain.

There was a cobbled slipway leading to the water's edge about
fifty yards away to my left. I ran along to it and made my way
down it to the sea. Acting on a kind of automatic pilot, I kicked
off my shoes, discarded my jacket and dived into the water. The
sea was Artic cold and for a few moments my body seized up
completely, the freezing water causing my limbs to lose their
ability to function. I thought my heart was about to burst out of

my chest and I cried out in shock, my voice disappearing into the dark night like a throaty whisper. It is moments like this that your natural survival instincts take over from the brain and body and, despite my fear and distress, I found myself striking out for the floating corpse.

I desperately tried to ignore the fierce penetrating cold and struggled on until I reached the body, though how I managed to do so, I'll never know. I managed to turn the body over and then, hooking my arms under him, I began to tug him back to the runway. Icy water sloshed into my mouth and I began to lose the feeling in my limbs, but some innate grim determination to survive drove me on. After all, what else could I do? I didn't want there to be two corpses floating in the sea. Eventually, I reached the runway and was able to haul the body onto the slimy cobbles. I took a few moments to recover, my chest rising and falling at a rapid rate. I slumped back and gazed at the stars, gasping for breath, wondering if my lungs would ever retain their normal rhythm. I waited a while until some feeble warmth returned to my shivering body and my breathing eased. Then, I leant over the body I had dragged from the murky deep and gazed at his face, which was ashen in the moonlight.

There was no doubt about it. This was Walter Clements, and he was dead. I could hardly believe it, despite the evidence before my eyes.

'So,' I said to myself, 'the story ends here.'

Of course I was wrong.

I was just about to stand up when I felt something press against the back of my neck. I am an experienced detective and have been in many a tight corner enough to realise that what was applying pressure to that part of my body was the barrel of a gun. To confirm this, I heard the click of the trigger being primed.

'What have you done, Johnny?' said a voice in the gloom behind me.

CHAPTER TWENTY SIX
From the journal of Johnny Hawke

When I was a naïve, inexperienced copper – a mere PC pounding the beat – I found myself in a similar situation while investigating a robbery at a warehouse. Some villain crept up behind me and stuck a pistol in my neck. In those days, when I had two functioning eyes, I thought that not only was I God's gift to policing, but I was a kind of sharp tough guy cast from the same mould as Sam Spade or Philip Marlowe. I had all the slick spiel and even slicker moves. It was a legacy of spending too much time at the pictures. So, with a swift, and what I considered a balletic movement, I pulled forward and dodged to the left. It wasn't the graceful move I had hoped for. I had stepped on my own foot and fell to the ground. However, it was a good job I did in this instance, for at that moment the creep fired the gun. My tumble meant that the bullet only missed me by inches. I was very lucky, but the incident taught me a lesson. Since then I've learned to be more cautious and less athletic in such situations.

Therefore, as I crouched over the inert body of Walter Clements with a gun pressing uncomfortably in the nape of my neck, I was not about to do anything dramatic. Besides, I recognised the voice of the gun's owner.

'Could I stand up?' I asked politely.

There was a brief pause before I received a reply. 'Easy does it.'

'Thank you, Susan.' I said. And then I took the risk of turning slowly to face her. 'If it is Susan; I reckon that's not your real name, is it?' I added gently as I faced the girl who had professed to be Frances Clements' sister.

Her face was stern in the moonlight, brow contracted and eyes hooded, but she still looked very attractive. What a shame she turned out to be an evil lady.

Nimbly, she moved the gun to aim at my chest. 'Why did you do it, Johnny?'

'Do what...?' I turned my head and glanced down at the wet corpse at my feet. 'You don't think...?' Despite everything, I found myself smiling. 'You don't think I killed this chap? What – pushed him into the water, saw him drown and then jumped in and pull him out again? That's a crazy idea.'

There was a flicker of uncertainty in her eyes as she rationalised the situation and realised that perhaps she had misjudged it.

'So, tell me what happened?'

'I came down here looking for our friend – and I found him, but he was floating face down in the briny. I did indeed jump in and pull him out, although I assumed that he was dead. Well, we still need a body, don't we? Look, there is quite a vicious gash on the back of the head. It's still bleeding. He was obviously slugged on land and the murderer hoped to consign him to a deep watery grave but I guess it's part of traitor's character that causes them to float.'

A ghost of a smile floated across her lips.

'Have you checked his clothing?' she asked.

'I was about to do that when I was rudely interrupted by having a gun poked in my neck. Are you going to put that away now or am I still your enemy?'

My question seemed to disquiet her.

'Are you working for the Russians?' I asked.

'Of course not.'

'Then who?'

'British Intelligence.'

'So why all the bloody secrecy? I am on your side.'

'You might be in principle but we were not sure of that. And besides, you're a meddling amateur. We couldn't let you go blundering about like a clumsy Sherlock Holmes...'

'Thank you very much.'

'I'm sorry, I didn't mean to be rude, but the truth is you're out of your depth, Johnny. This is not a simple case of homicide; this involves national security. Even the police are not involved.'

'Well, one way or another you've got your man.'

'The man was the least of our problems.'

'What do you mean?'

'It's what he has that is the real prize.'

'What he has? What has he?'

'Let's search his clothing and find out.'

'I'll do it,' I said, stooping down again. 'I am familiar with men's apparel.' I grinned but it had no effect. 'What am I looking for exactly?'

'I am not quite sure.'

'Oh, that's great.'

'Just shut up and check his clothes for any items.'

I did so. My hands wriggled in and out of the sodden clothing but discovered nothing. There was no wallet, cigarette case, lighter, coins, comb – zilch. I conveyed the bad news to my companion and she swore.

'OK lady, I think it's time to spill the beans what you – what *we* are looking for. I've come all this way with you, I think I deserve to know.'

Susan (or whatever her name was) gave a heavy sigh. 'Very well, I suppose there's no harm now. Walter Clements worked as a clerk at the War Office. Quite a lowly position really, but he did have access to sensitive information. The stuff that he has been slipping the Soviets has been trivial. We've even been able to provide him with false bits of info which has helped to put the enemy on the back foot which was a great benefit for us. We have been monitoring our Walter for quite some time. However, his masters encouraged him to be more ambitious. They didn't want just titbits any more, they wanted something really substantial.'

'Like what?'

'Like a list of the names and addresses of all the allied agents living in the USSR and Europe.'

I whistled.

'With that list in their hands, they could wipe out our network of agents at a stroke. Then we would be blind – that's the term we use. It would shift the balance of power very much in their favour. The icicles in this cold war would grow larger and sharper and the Siberian blast would be blowing in our direction.'

I nodded. 'And Walter has this list.'

'Well, he photographed it on microfilm but he managed to slip through our fingers before we were able to apprehend him.'

I was puzzled. 'You mean the Russians have got the film?'

'No. When Clements knew that the game was up, he did a bunk rather than hand it over. He obviously worked out that once they had the film and the fact that we were on to him, the Russians would eliminate him immediately. After all, he couldn't have worked for them for all that time without learning some of their secrets. It was in their interest to silence him before we got hold of him and he spilt all their beans in exchange for a lighter sentence.'

'One way of escaping the rope, I suppose.'

'The problem now is where the hell is that film.'

'Surely he would have kept it in on his person. There was no point in hiding it somewhere if he was doing a bunk to France.'

Susan nodded. 'But it's not on his person.'

'Therefore,' I continued, 'it seems to me the only explanation for its disappearance is that whoever bonked our friend on the head and dropped him into the sea has it.'

Susan nodded again, her features grim in the pale moonlight. 'I can't see how the Russians could get to him so quickly. Their two agents were killed in the crash.'

'I know but who else would want to murder the devil, and what for?'

'Perhaps it was a simple case of robbery. His pockets are empty.'

'A bit dramatic for whatever Clements had on him.'

'Well, his wallet's gone, and his watch. Remember he hoped he was heading for a new life on the continent. No doubt his wallet would be full of cash.'

'I suppose what you say makes sense, if a little optimistic,' I said. 'If that is the case, it's most likely that our perpetrator doesn't know what he's got.'

'Yes. The microfilm could be concealed in anything small: a box of matches, the stem of a pipe – even in the lining of his wallet.'

'Well, if it ain't the Russians that we're after, it's most likely someone local. A chancer.'

'What do you mean "that *we're* after?"'

'Oh, for Heaven's sake, don't start pulling government rank on me. And put that gun away. You're not going to shoot me in cold blood, are you? That's not the British way. I'm no threat to you. We're on the same side, and it seems to me we're also in the same sinking ship. If we don't join forces and act together it could easily be glug glug for both of us.'

'I suppose you are right, but let's get this clear – I'm in charge. What I say goes.'

'Yes, ma'am.' I gave her a sloppy salute to lighten the moment, but if she thought I was about to be bossed around by her, she was very much mistaken. It served my purposes for the moment to let her believe that I was taking on the role of an obedient puppy but I'd been too long in this game to play second fiddle.

'What now, then?' I asked.

She glanced down at the wet corpse. 'I've got to get in touch with my contact and pass on the news of Clements' death and arrange for his body to be picked up. We need a telephone.'

'Well, there's a pub in the village. No doubt they'll have a phone and I can dry off a bit and grab a glass of brandy to ward off the chill.'

'Brandy,' she sneered. 'Oh, yes, Johnny, get your priorities right. OK, we'll head for the pub, but first, we've got to do something with our friend here. We can't just leave him on the slipway.'

'There's a shelter up about a hundred yards away on the quayside. We can stow him there for the moment. He'll be out of sight 'til morning at least.'

And so that's what we did. I hauled the wet corpse up to the shelter and hid him under the wooden bench inside. He fitted in so snugly that you could hardly see him in the shadows.

That mission accomplished, we headed for the pub.

On entering The Crown and Anchor, we found the place empty apart from the barman who was just placing towels on the beer pumps.

'We're closed,' he snarled with an angry twist of his features which contained the added unspoken message of 'bugger off!'

'We need a drink and the use of your phone,' said Susan, her voice harsh and commanding as she strode up to the counter and faced the barman.

'Hardlines. We're closed.'

'I am in this area on government business and it is your duty to assist us.'

'And I am the king of China. Push off, lady.'

'Here is my official warrant card,' Susan said, holding it up before him.

He barely glanced at it. 'Makes no difference to me. It's just a piece of cardboard with printing on it.'

'Very well,' said Susan, replacing the card in her pocket. 'I can see that you need more proof of my authority.' She pulled out her pistol and aimed it at the barman. 'This satisfy you, mister?'

There was a dramatic change in the truculent barman's expression and demeanour. He took one step back, his face paling and his eyes widening. 'Whoa, lady I... I meant no harm. Don't hurt me.'

'We're not here to hurt you, you idiot. All we're after is some civility along with two large brandies and the use of your telephone.'

'Yeah, yeah, brandies OK lady.... Coming up.' With shaking hands, he retrieved a bottle and two glasses from the shelf behind him and began pouring. 'I'm sorry but I can't oblige with the telephone, miss. You see, we ain't got one. There isn't one in the village. The line only reaches to Littlehampton. We were promised one after the war but they haven't got round to it yet.' He gave a twisted smile, which was more unpleasant than his angry face.

Susan and I exchanged gloomy looks. That was a blow.

'Have you had a stranger in here tonight?' I asked. 'Thickset chap with blonde hair and probably wearing glasses.'

'Yes,' the barman nodded, pleased to be helping the lady with the gun. 'Yes, there was such a chap. He was wanting to hire a boat. He asked me if there was someone who could help him.'

'And what did you say?'

'I pointed out Sam Brewer, one of my regulars; he's always up for earning some extra cash. He was sitting over there by the fire with old Joe.'

'Go on. Did the blonde chap approach this Brewer?'

'Yes, he did. After a few moments, they went into a huddle. I saw this chap pass money to Sam.'

'As though a deal had been struck?'

'Looked that way.'

'What happened then?'

'Brewer skedaddled out of here quick sticks and the blonde guy bought another drink. He stayed a while, then left.'

'What do you know of this Sam Brewer?'

'He's a local fisherman. Has a small boat called the Aurora.'

'Is it berthed down by the quay?'

'Yes, usually.'

'Is he a decent bloke?' asked Susan.

The barman hesitated.

'Come on,' she said, waving the pistol at him.

'Well, I have heard that he gets involved in some shady deals.'

'Such as?' she asked.

'Smuggling stuff.'

'Like good brandy,' I said, raising my glass.

For a brief moment, the barman turned away, somewhat shamefacedly.

'Don't worry we're not interested in how you manage to stock your shelves. Where does this Brewer live?'

'On his boat, of course.'

'The Aurora.'

'Yes.'

Susan and I exchanged glances. We each knew what the other was thinking. We both knew it was time to see if we could have a word with this dubious character.

'Let's drink up, shall we,' I said to Susan.

She had anticipated me and had drained her glass.

CHAPTER TWENTY SEVEN
From the journal of Johnny Hawke

Leaving our favourite barman, the one who pours enormous measures of brandy and doesn't charge for them, we made our way back towards the quay once more in search of the little fishing boat called Aurora and, in particular, its owner Sam Brewer.

'Are you thinking what I'm thinking'? said Susan.

'That I'd like another glass of that contraband brandy...'

She gave a short sigh of annoyance. 'You know what I mean.'

'Yes. That it's very likely that this chap Brewer took Mr Clements for a ride. But not on his boat. He agreed to sail him to France but clocked him over the head instead and took all his cash and his other possessions.'

'Including the microfilm.'

'But if he's just a local small-time villain, he'll have no idea what he's got his hands on.'

'That doesn't help us a lot.'

'Indeed. If it's secreted in some ordinary little item like a cigarette packet or something mundane like that, it could be that Brewer has got rid of it as being no use to him at all. He may well have ditched it overboard.'

Susan groaned. 'Don't say that.'

We walked along the quay looking carefully at all the boats, and it wasn't long before we came upon the neat little vessel with the name Aurora in faded letters on the side. There was a faint glimmer of light emanating from the cabin and, to our surprise, the sound of voices. We crept on deck and listened. I could not hear what was being said, but I was able to determine that there were two men involved in lively conversation.

'I'll go in and confront them,' I whispered. 'You stay out here with your little gun in readiness to prevent either of them making a bunk for it.'

To my surprise, Susan accepted my suggestion without question and just nodded. I stepped down the few stairs and tested the handle the cabin door. It wasn't locked and, taking a deep breath, I made my entrance. Coming into the cabin illuminated by one oil lamp dangling from the low ceiling, I saw two men sitting around a table each with a glass of what I assumed was brandy, no doubt of the contraband sort. On the table was a collection of items laid out carefully as though for examination. At the side of these was a neat pile of crisp white five-pound notes. The men had been in animated chatter when I entered, but now turning their gaze in my direction, their cheerful faced darkened instantly, surprised at this sudden intrusion.

'What the hell?' cried one and rose to his feet.

'Calm yourself, gentlemen. This is just a friendly visit,' I said.

'Get off my boat,' the man said.

'Ah, so you must be Mr Sam Brewer. Perhaps you'll be kind enough to introduce me to your fellow conspirator.'

The other man also rose to his feet in an unsteady fashion. Well, that brandy was pretty potent. 'I'll bloody well introduce myself,' he growled and attempted to throw a punch in my direction. It went wide of its target and he stumbled forward, allowing me the opportunity to return the compliment and punch him hard in the face. My fist connected with force on his chin. He wobbled unsteadily while still managing to maintain an erect posture but the blurry eyes indicated that he didn't know quite what had hit him. *It was me, pal*, I thought. And to prove it, I hit him again with such power that this time he collapsed in an unconscious heap. While this was happening, Brewer had left his chair at the far side of the table and was heading for me. As he grew nearer, the cabin door opened and Susan entered. Suddenly, there was a loud explosion and a dark crimson mark materialised in the middle of Brewer's forehead. A thin trickle of blood began running down towards his eyes which were wide with shock and horror. His slack mouth champed silently while he hung there for a few moments as though he was suspended on invisible wires, before dropping to the ground.

I turned to Susan, who was holding her gun firmly before her.

'My God,' I cried, 'you've killed him!'

'Yes. Of course, what else was I expected to do?'

I shook my head in wild bewilderment. How the bloody hell was I supposed to answer such a question? This wasn't the timid damsel in distress I'd first met. This was a trigger-happy heartless bitch. 'I could have dealt with him,' I said at length, my voice raspy and thin. 'There was no need... no need to kill the man.'

Susan shrugged. 'He's no loss. He's a crook and probably a murderer.'

'Isn't that for a judge and jury to decide?'

'We have simply speeded up the process.'

'No 'we' haven't! Don't include me in your crazy action.'

'You're rather a sensitive flower, aren't you Johnny? Are you sure you're in the right business?'

I've never hit a woman or, in fact, ever felt the desire to do so, but at that moment, I wanted to wallop her hard across the kisser. I didn't, of course. Such violence would solve nothing and would only bring me down to her grimy level. Instead, I just glowered at her. It was, I was aware, a fairly pathetic response but any other meaningful words or actions failed me.

She looked at the items arranged neatly on the table; the sundry spoils of Brewer and his friend's crime. She gave a quick smile and moved closer to examine then. It was obviously stuff belonging to Clements. There was the wallet, some coins, a wristwatch, a pack of cigarettes, a box of matches, a packet of chewing gum and a St Christopher's medal.

Susan leaned over the table and snatched up the matchbox. 'I think this is it,' she said, almost to herself. 'I need a knife,' she added. She gazed around the cramped cabin and saw there was a penknife resting on a shelf by the door. Snatching it up, she beckoned me forward under the oil lamp hanging above the table. 'I've seen this technique before. It's a fairly common method of transporting documents in microfilm form, and very clever.'

Carefully, she applied the blade of the knife to the sandpaper strip on the matchbox, inserting the tip under the edge. She slowly prised the strip free and then, slowly and gently, she pulled the strip away from the box so that it curled like a sandy tongue adhering to one end of the box, exposing the thin cardboard layer beneath.

'Look,' she said, holding the box closer to me.

I did look. Catching the light were two glistening objects which appeared to be tiny squares of gelatine slipped into fine slits in the cardboard. They were, no doubt two frames of microfilm, little beauties that all this twisted drama had been all about. It was the miniature record of the spy network that must not find its way into the dangerous mitts of the Russians.

'Let me see,' I said, taking the box from Susan and holding it up to my face for closer examination.

'Bloody hell,' I said. 'That's amazing.' Such was my excitement that my fingers shook and the box almost fell to the floor.

'You oaf,' cried my companion.

'Old butterfingers, me,' I smiled inanely.

'Give it to me,' Susan demanded, her voice edged with a dark threat.

Securing the sandpaper strip back in place, I passed the box over. 'I suppose you consider that your mission has been successful, despite four corpses,' I said.

'Of course. We have what we wanted. That overrides any other consideration. What you may regard as an unfortunate casualty is of no consequence.'

'My, my, but you are a cold lady.'

'I wouldn't be any good at my job if I wasn't.'

'You don't work for the British Security service, do you? All that guff you told me earlier was just a pack of lies.'

There was a brief flicker of amusement in her eyes. 'Ah, you're beginning to see daylight at last, eh, Johnny? I wondered how long it would take for the rouble to drop.'

'It dropped a while ago. I just wanted us to find the microfilm together.'

'Well, now we have and I've got it.' She held up the matchbox as though it was a sporting trophy. 'So, now, there is just one thing left for me to do.'

The sense of danger in the air had grown toxic. I didn't need further prompting. As she raised her pistol and aimed it at me, I jumped sideways and smashed my fist against the oil lamp dangling above us. It crashed down on the table, plunging the room into darkness. I leapt forward and pushed Susan to the ground. She fired her gun but, thankfully, the bullet came nowhere near me. Jumping over her I wrenched open the cabin door and clambered up the steps onto the deck. As I did so, another shot rang out. This one was much closer for comfort. She was on my tail. Her next shot would likely be more accurate. I knew there was only one thing I could do now to affect a successful escape. With just a modicum of hesitation, I jumped off the side of the boat into the dark icy water once more. Crikey, I was making a habit of this.

It's strange, but in one of the comics I read as a kid when a character fell into water, the cartoonist would bubble the word 'Splosh!' Well, I seemed to drop into the icy sea with that exact sound – a sound that was followed by a gunshot and a bullet that pipped the water only a few inches from my head.

Despite the fierce cold and all-embracing fear I felt, I dived under the surface and swam as fast as I could away from the boat. Thank goodness it was night and she couldn't see clearly in which direction I was headed. Determination and a dogged survival instinct kept me going. Besides, I wasn't going to let her get the better of me – the bloody traitor. So I set my brain and my body into mechanical mode and just swam. The problem was that I had become disorientated and had no idea where I was or what direction to take. Before my lungs burst, I broke the surface and gazed around me. I couldn't see the shore. All around me was blackness and the gentle heave of freezing water.

What the hell was I to do? Which way was I supposed to swim?

CHAPTER TWENTY EIGHT

Barnes entered the inner sanctum after politely knocking twice. He was allowed access because he had been fully vetted and scrutinised by those in charge of this highly secret and dangerous network of agents embedded like fault lines in Britain. And he had been in service for his master for over twenty years. Sir Jeremy was in conversation with a stout man who was smoking a large cigar. He wore an expensive tweed suit; the buttons of his waistcoat were straining to break free from his more than ample stomach. The two men were peering at a document set out on Sir Jeremy's desk. Barnes knew the man. He was a regular visitor – part of the team - though he had to admit to himself that he did not care for the fellow. He was arrogant and condescending and, as Barnes saw it, completely charmless. On top of that, he was rather a common fellow.

'What is it, Barnes?' said Sir Jeremy, looking up from the document.

'You have a visitor, sir. Miss Smith.'

Sir Jeremy's features brightened. 'Really! By George, that's wonderful. Do send her straight in. I have been so worried about her.'

'Immediately, sir.'

Moments later, a young woman entered. She was tall, pretty, with remarkably penetrating eyes.

Sir Jeremy moved forward to embrace her. 'Elsa, my dear, it is so good to see you.'

She smiled and planted a gentle kiss on the man's cheek. 'The feeling is mutual.'

'You know Roland Sanders, of course.'

She nodded. 'Hello. How is the washing machine business?'

The plump man gave a fixed smile and tapped the ash of his cigar into a large glass ashtray on the desk. 'Running smoothly – as you might expect,' he announced grandly. 'You have news of this Clements affair.'

'Yes, I do,' she replied.

'Let me get you a drink, my dear,' said Sir Jeremy, 'and then you can tell us all about it. G and T is your tipple isn't it, Elsa?'

'That would be lovely.'

'I suspect you'd like another, Roland.'

'That's right,' came the tart reply.

Once the drinks were supplied the two men sat on a large ottoman while Ella placed herself opposite them in a winged armchair.

'Now, my dear, do tell all. I am most concerned to learn about your exploits and, in particular, their outcome. This is so important to us.'

'Of course. I will provide all the precise details of my mission in my report, so for the moment, I will just give you the general outline of how things progressed.'

'Go ahead, my dear,' said Sir Jeremy.

'Well, to begin with, I had no difficulty in convincing John Hawke that I was Frances Clements' sister. He accepted me in that role without question. In many ways, he was easy to manipulate and I had no difficulty persuading him to let me accompany him on his investigations. He was a useful tool and bright enough to pick up Clements' trail.'

Sir Jeremy nodded. 'We knew this, of course, from the reports that Olga and Basil were able to pass on to us. They were able to keep a close tag on you until… their unfortunate accident.'

'Indeed. You know then that we encountered Clements at a roadhouse. There was a kind of confrontation with Hawke. He is rather the proverbial bull in a china shop. Clements managed to escape in the process and I allowed him, almost persuaded him to take me as a hostage.' At this juncture she allowed herself a brief smile before continuing. 'I was hoping I could find a way of retrieving the microfilm. It was frustrating having him so close to me and yet not be able to do anything until I had discovered where the microfilm was. I had no idea how or where he had concealed it. I was playing for time. He was driving like a bat out of that dark place, desperate to put as many miles between himself and Hawke as he could. At this point, I did not know that we were being trailed by Olga and Basil but I did see what happened to them. It was very unpleasant.'

'It is one of the downsides of our dangerous game,' observed Sir Jeremy. 'One doesn't sign up expecting a cosy life.'

Elsa nodded and had a sip of her gin before she continued. 'By this time, I had managed to get away from Clements. The situation was too dangerous for me. I could not establish where the microfilm was or how I could retrieve it. I was aware that Clements, desperate as he was, could shoot me at any time. I had to bail out at this juncture and employ another tactic. I had already established that Hawke had worked out that Clements was headed for the little fishing village of Clovelly Bay, beyond Littlehampton, where he had hopes of securing a boat that would take him to France. That's where I caught up with Hawke and he had caught up with Clements – after a fashion.'

Sir Jeremy did not interrupt Elsa's flow, but at this juncture, raised a gentle quizzical eyebrow.

Elsa explained: 'Clements had done a deal with a fellow he met in the local pub who apparently had agreed to ferry him to France – for a price. It was, in the end, a very large price. Clements paid for it with his life.'

'The fellow is dead then?

'Yes. It was an act of robbery. I don't think this sailor man meant to kill Clements. He was probably just over-eager to get his hands on his cash. Whatever… he slugged Clements hard. The blow did for him. And so sailor man ditched his body in the sea.'

'Great heavens. With the microfilm? Then we are lost.'

Elsa shook her head. 'No, before dumping his body into the water, this fellow extracted all the items from Clements' clothing, including a certain matchbox.'

'A matchbox. Is that of particular interest?' Sir Jeremy's eyes gleamed with curiosity, as his mind raced ahead of the game.

'So it turned out. It was John Hawke who dragged Clements' corpse out of the sea. Ironically, it was with his help that we managed to track down the sailor man and his mate on their little boat. There was a scuffle and both men ended up dead. I shot them both.'

'They are of little consequence,' observed Sanders with a sneer. 'What about the microfilm?'

'I'm coming to that. Sailor man and his crony had gathered all the items that Clements had on him in the cabin on his boat, including his wallet, of course. Amongst the stuff was a matchbox. Now I've seen these used before to convey information, inserting microdots or film under the emery strip. A box of matches is such an innocent-looking thing. Most of us carry one. They are taken for granted. As I say, innocent.'

'But not this one, eh?' Sir Jeremy observed.

'No, not this one, said Elsa with a smile. 'Pulling back the emery strip, I discovered two minute squares of celluloid; the vital microfilm.'

Sir Jeremy clapped his hands. 'Excellent.'

'What about Hawke?' asked Sanders.

'Well, whatever his usefulness to us, it was over.'

'Excellent,' Sanders grinned. 'So you killed him.'

Elsa paused and pursed her lips. 'In a manner of speaking.'

'What do you mean?' asked Sir Jeremy.

'Before I could carry out the execution, he read my thoughts and sensed what I intended to do. Just as I was about to shoot him, he knocked me down and made a bolt for it. We were on the boat at the time and he ran up on deck and dived into the sea. I fired after him and I'm fairly certain that I hit him but, if I didn't, he certainly couldn't have lasted for long in that icy water. The fellow's dead all right. I'm just sorry I can't provide a corpse.'

'As long as he's out of the picture, that's all that matters. That and the matchbox, of course.'

Elsa reached into her handbag. 'I have it here,' she said, holding it up like a stage magician.

Both men beamed and leaned forward to observe it more closely.

'It certainly looks like an ordinary matchbox,' said Sir Jeremy.

'But one containing treasure trove.,' said Elsa.

'Please demonstrate.'

Elsa slipped her fingernail under the edge of the emery strip to loosen it and peeled it back. As she did so, she let out a gasp of horror.

147

'What is it?' asked Sir Jeremy.

'There's nothing there. The two frames of microfilm have gone.'

'Gone!' Sir Jeremy rose from his chair, a mixture of anger and bewilderment clouding his features. 'What on earth do you mean? Perhaps they have slipped out into your bag.'

Elsa shook her head. 'No, no, they were secured by tiny slits in the cardboard.'

'But…how could they have disappeared?'

And then the thought came to her in a vivid flash. John Hawke. Of course, when he handled the box in a clumsy fashion: 'Old butterfingers'! He must have… The bastard! She had been so stupid not to check. Indeed, in the end, she had proved to be the clumsy one. The microfilm was at the bottom of the English Channel, along with John Hawke.

She gazed in dismay at Sir Jeremy. He loured over her, his growing anger colouring his cheeks. He was waiting for an explanation. There was nothing she could do but tell the truth. Any other explanation would not ring true. And she couldn't lie to him. Apart from her sense of loyalty and devotion, he knew her too well. He could detect a lie immediately – especially from her. She also knew now that whatever she said, she was going to be in hot water. She almost smiled at that childish phrase. It hardly covered what punishment she was likely to face. To have failed in such a crucial assignment was tantamount to treason.

'Well,' she began, 'It looks like…' And haltingly, she recounted the incident concerning Hawke and the matchbox.

When she had finished, Sir Jeremy slapped his forehead in angry frustration but said nothing. Sanders, however, could not resist a coarse, 'Stupid bitch.'

Sir Jeremy turned to him swiftly and seemed to be on the verge of issuing a rebuke, but thought better of it. Instead, he placed his hand on Sanders' shoulder. 'Perhaps you could leave us alone for a while, Roland. I need to deal with this situation… with discretion. I am sure you understand.'

Sanders' expression clearly indicated that he did understand, but was reluctant to go. He wanted to hear what Sir Jeremy was going to say to the stupid cow.

'There are... complications.' Sir Jeremy glanced at Elsa who was staring straight ahead of her as though she was not part of this scene at all. For the moment, her mind was numb.

With a gentle press on the shoulders, Sir Jeremy directed Sanders to the door.

Once he had left, Sir Jeremy turned to Elsa with a heavy sigh.

'Now, my girl, this is a pretty pickle you've got yourself into,' he said.

CHAPTER TWENTY NINE

Toby, the young and energetic fox terrier, pulled heartily on the lead. His owner, Ralph Brooke, tugged him back. 'Do behave, you scamp,' he said easily. 'Let's get to the beach before you start getting frisky.'

The sun was just rising and the rich yellow strands of sunlight which fanned out on the grey rolling waters promised a good day. Man and terrier made their way to the shingle and once there, Ralph released Toby from the lead and the dog raced off to the water's edge as though his life depended upon it. Ralph could not help but smile at this display of exuberance. *How wonderful*, he thought*, to get such joy from such simple pleasures*. Well, he got just as much enjoyment from taking the dog down to the beach twice a day and watching him cavort along the shore. That was a simple pleasure, too. Toby was the best thing that had happened to him since Betty, his wife, died and he was grateful for the companionship of the unruly mutt.

He lit a cigarette and gazed out to sea, remembering the times he and Betty came for walks down here. His reverie was interrupted by a fusillade of loud barking. He saw that Toby was circling a dark shape on the shore and announcing his interest.

'What have you found now,' murmured Ralph to himself as he stepped on to the shingle and crunched his way towards the dog and the source of his excitement. As he grew nearer he saw, to his alarm, that the dark shape appeared to be a body – the body of a man lying face downwards.

'My God,' he said as he quickened his pace. Toby rushed forward to greet him. 'OK boy, let me look,' he said pulling the dog away from the body. The man's clothes were sopping wet, so it was obvious that he had been in the sea. Slowly, he turned the body over. It was a youngish man, somewhere in his thirties with a strong face, wearing a black eyepatch over his left eye. Ralph felt for the man's pulse. It was there, but only just – a faint irregular rhythm.

'What a miracle. The feller's alive, Toby. We've got to get

him to a hospital as soon as possible. If he doesn't receive proper medical attention soon, I reckon he'll be a goner.'

Toby gave a bark of agreement.

CHAPTER THIRTY

Elsa finished dabbing her moist eyes and accepted the glass of sherry proffered by Sir Jeremy. She took a sip and emitted a huge shy. 'Oh, Daddy, I've made a right pig's ear of it, haven't I?'

'I am afraid you have, my dear. You did brilliantly at first, but you fell at the final furlong and that negates all your previous efforts and early success. It places me in a very difficult position. The men who run this section are not going to let you get away without punishment. Being my daughter will carry no weight with them. In losing that microfilm, you have failed spectacularly, and they are not going to take very kindly to it.'

'What will they do?'

Sir Jeremy shook his head and strode to the fireplace and turned his back on Elsa. He appeared to be gazing at the oil painting hanging over the mantelpiece. 'I don't know. I am fearful, though. They could take you to Russia and install you in one of their offices there, or they could...' His voice faded away. He turned slowly and gazed at his daughter, his features drawn and bleak.

'They could have me eliminated,' she said softly, finishing his sentence.

'You know too much, you see. You know their rules; no second chances.'

'What must I do?'

'We'll have to get you away, out of the country, pronto. You'll just have to disappear. Lose yourself abroad. I can trust Barnes to make the arrangements and you'll have to say goodbye to England for a good long while, possibly forever.'

Elsa rose and threw her arm around her father. 'Oh, Dad, I can't bear it.'

He kissed her gently on the cheek. 'Of course you can. You are a spy. You have been trained to survive and you will – but you will be on your own. To stay in this country would be suicide. It is not just the Soviets who will be after you now. The

British police and security services will be looking for the young woman who accompanied John Hawke in his investigations and murdered two men. England is too hot for you. The sooner you get to Europe, the better. You have languages, knowhow and courage. You will survive.'

'But what about you?'

He gave her a gentle smile and shrugged. 'I, too, will survive. I haven't made a mess of things – I left that to my daughter. But my privileged connections with the government and those in high places give me security. They will still need my ... assistance. I still remain useful to them.'

'But I won't ever see you again.' She began to cry now.

'Oh, no, my dear, don't say that. I feel sure that at some point in the future...' He broadened his smile but Elsa knew that smile, it was empty and false. It told her in no uncertain terms that this was the final goodbye.

CHAPTER THIRTY ONE
From the journal of Johnny Hawke

Was it Christmas? Glittering fairy lights and snowflakes seemed to be dancing around me. Splinters of light pierced the darkness of my cocoon. Gradually, I emerged into this unfamiliar bright atmosphere as though I was newly born. I was now aware of my body and the stirring of my limbs. I also became conscious of some sort of feeling. It wasn't a pleasant feeling. What was it? Ah, yes, now I recognised it. It was pain. Perhaps discomfort would be a better description. Gosh, I was able to play about with language. My brain must be waking up and making judgements. This discomfort was concentrated somewhere in my body. I blinked my eyes and the splinters of light grew brighter. Ah, yes – that pain or discomfort I now was able to recognise as a headache. But not such a headache as I had experienced before. It was as if someone was drilling a hole in my skull.

Tangible shapes began to appear and my growing awareness told me consciousness was returning. Where the hell it had been, I had no idea. But then, in my current state, ideas were still in their embryo stage. Thinking was a new process. Who I was, where I was – these were questions hanging in the ether above my head – the one which was afflicted with discomfort.

Suddenly, I began to cough and splutter as though my throat was ready to reassert itself after lying dormant for a while. Two shapes approached me and hauled me up into a sitting position. They gradually came into focus. Nurses. Memory recognised their uniforms. Lovely, fresh-faced nurses. Of course, now it became clear to me: I was in hospital. Slowly, the misty clouds parted and the brain cleared even more and fragments of memory filtered through. Then, I remembered the water and the dark and the bitter cold and the blackness that engulfed me. The blackness I surrendered to. My God, that was it! The memory reasserted itself, sharp as a knife. I had nearly drowned. But obviously, I hadn't, unless this was some kind of alternative heaven.

One of the nurses held a glass of water to my lips. 'Take a few sips of this,' she said softly, her voice having a pleasing Irish lilt. I did as I was told. 'That's a good boy,' she said. 'Take your time; see if you can empty the glass.' I could and I did. This water was divine…unlike…

'Now then, my lad,' said my Irish angel in a brisk business-like fashion, 'do you think you could manage a bowl of broth?'

'Yes, please,' I said eagerly, my voice emerging a gruff whisper as though my tonsils were rattling. It was as if I had just learned to talk.

'I'll bring it to you directly,' she said and both nurses departed the room. As they did so, I heard one of them speak someone outside in the corridor. 'Not yet. It's too soon. You've got to give him more time.'

While I waited for my broth, I made a determined effort to clear away the remaining fog from my brain and piece together the history of my recent days. After a sluggish start, I began to remember everything, until that moment when I jumped in the sea and began swimming for my life. After that, things were a blank. Somehow, I had survived and landed up in a hospital somewhere. How long I had been here and what had happened to Susan were questions that still required answers.

The Irish nurse returned with a bowl of thin-looking soup, but it was warm and had a pleasingly salty taste.

'That will do you good,' she smiled. 'Can you manage a spoon?'

'Let me try.' I did, and could. That cheered me more than I can say. *I'm starting to function again*, I told myself. Spoon today. Knife and fork tomorrow.

While spooning my way through the broth I asked the nurse, 'Tell me, where am I? What hospital is this?'

'Maidstone General'

'How did I get here?

'By ambulance, of course.'

I smiled. Of course. 'But where did I come from?'

'You were found on the beach in Clovelly Bay. You were half dead, my lad. It's a wonder you're still here and able to take the broth.'

Then the thought struck me. I cursed my tired brain for not thinking of it before. 'Where are my clothes?' I asked; there was more urgency in my tone than I intended and it caused the nurse to raise her eyebrows in response.

'Oh, they're quite safe, my lad. You don't go worrying about such things at the moment. You won't be wanting them in a hurry.'

'I just want to know where they are.'

'In there.' She pointed to the locker by the side of my bed.

I tried to hide my relief and nodded gently before returning to the broth.

'That's good', I said after emptying the bowl. 'I'm feeling more like my old self.'

'Ah, but you've quite a way to go yet before you're back to your real old self. You're still quite weak.'

I laughed. 'Not me. I'm fit as a fiddle – an old creaky fiddle, I admit, but I can still come up with a tune.'

She gave me an indulgent smile. 'Then you'll be up to receiving visitors? There are some gentlemen outside who have been waiting patiently to see you. They seem very concerned about you.'

'Well, send them in. I should like to see them.'

Without a word, she took the bowl and hastened to the door and waved in my visitors before scurrying off down the corridor.

Three men approached the bed. One I knew of old. It was David Llewellyn. He was the only one who was grinning. It warmed my heart to see him. The other men looked grim, as though they were attending a funeral. One was a burly man in a large tweed overcoat. His eyes were rather frightening, bulging out from beneath large bushy eyebrows. The other man was in a grey belted raincoat, clasping a bowler hat. He was pale, with high cheekbones and a small, rather miserable mouth.

'How are you feeling, boyo?' asked David cheerily.

'Slowly returning back to the land of the living' I said in my new croaky ghost of a voice.

My eyes shifted to the two strangers. 'And who have we

here?' I asked, although I had a fairly good idea.

'We're from National Security, Mr Hawke', said Bushy Eyebrows. 'It's good to see you're on the road to recovery.'

'Thank you for your concern,' I said.

He ignored my sarcasm. 'I suspect you know why we're here. You have been treading on our toes in recent days, involving yourself in matters that really do not concern you.'

'I would beg to differ, but I'll need another bowl of soup to give me the energy to dispute your statement.'

'Mr Hawke, I will not beat about the bush. You know all about the item that we wish to retrieve before it falls into the wrong hands. We believe that you know its whereabouts.'

'Do I?'

'Now is not the time to play games, Mr Hawke,' he said sourly.

'Can you vouch for these fellows, David?'

He nodded. 'They're legit.'

'What if I was to tell you that the girl Susan has the microfilm...'

The two men exchanged worried glances. Their discomfort pleased me tremendously.

I hitched myself up further in the bed. 'David, will you reach into the locker down there and bring out my jacket?'

He did as I asked without a word and passed it to me. It was still quite damp and smelt of the sea. It struck me inconsequently that I would never want to wear this jacket again; not just because of its reek of the brine, but also because of the dark memories it carried with it. I pulled the jacket across my lap and prayed that my little Houdini moment was going to work as I dug my hand into the right-hand side pocket. My fingers searched the slimy interior. To my surprise, there was nothing there. My God, there was nothing there! My heart sank and my throat grew very dry again, the benefit of the soup evaporating on the instant. I gazed up at the three faces who were watching me intently.

In desperation, I investigated further and, praise be, my forefinger caught on something sharp. I scooped it up and brought it out of the pocket. My lips curled into a grin as I saw that what I had retrieved were the two frames of microfilm stuck together by the damp. I held them out in the palm of my hand.

'I believe this is what you are looking for, gentlemen,' I said with a grin of triumph.

The two men rushed forward and stared at the two little gelatine frames bonded by damp as though they were priceless gems – which in a way, I suppose they were.

The two men smiled and I could see that this was the use of a rare facial expression for both of them. I beamed, too. I had – in the end – achieved my Houdini moment. Ted Der!

Then, in an instant, Bushy Eyebrows had scooped up the microfilm frames and, observing an ashtray on top of my locker, dropped them into it.

'What on earth are you doing?' I cried.

His gloomy-faced associate extracted a box of matches from his raincoat pocket and struck one. It flared into orange life. 'Making sure no unfriendly hands get hold of these,' he said as he dropped the match into the ashtray. The microfilm flared into flames immediately and was quickly turned into a minute pile of grey dust.

David chuckled. 'I told you, gentlemen, that my pal Johnny was the man who would get you what you want.'

'We appreciate his efforts in this matter, but if he hadn't interfered, things may have been somewhat simpler,' said Bushy Eyebrows, his voice as cutting as a guillotine. 'And maybe we could have got our hands-on of the girl, too. Now she has gone to ground and there is little hope that we will ever be able to find her.'

'Well,' I said pointedly, my own spirits rising once more, 'that is probably down to your incompetence. As for me interfering, as you so nicely put it, I was carrying out my own murder investigation and your intrigue just got in the way. And may I remind you that if it hadn't been for me, that microfilm could be in France now.'

'Don't pat yourself too hard on the back, Mr Hawke. We haven't done with you yet. When you are well enough to return to London we shall need to hold a debriefing session with you. We want to hear the full story of your colourful escapades.'

With this parting shot, both men turned in mechanical unison and left the room.

'Arrogant bastards,' growled David.

'It comes with the territory, I suppose,' I said, smiling.

'Yes, boyo, and with the breeding.'

'So there is no sign of Susan or whatever her real name is?'

David shook his head. 'As you know, they've kept me mainly in the dark, telling me little. I'm only here because of you and our connection. They treat the police as idiots as though we have no idea how to deal with crime, whatever its nature or origin. Perhaps our country would not be in such a perilous situation because of the cold war if they'd involve us more, allowing us to share their responsibilities. They cannot see that their tight arses are part of the problem.'

I agreed with David, but I couldn't rally to the cause because suddenly I began to feel sleepy and my brain began to grow cloudy. It seems my Irish nurse had been right – I had a way to go before I was back to my old self.

I slumped back on my pillow, exhausted with what just happened in the last ten minutes. With relief, I closed my eyes. 'I'm sorry,' I murmured. Before I could say any more, fatigue overtook me and I fell asleep.

CHAPTER THIRTY TWO
From the journal of Johnny Hawke

It was five days before I was allowed out of hospital, but by then, I had recovered most of my strength and mental agility – as much as I ever had, anyway. As I stepped outside the hospital and breathed in fresh air once again, I momentarily felt dizzy and intoxicated. It was so strange after the dull dry air of the hospital ward. As I waited for my senses to readjust to the real world, a black sedan drew up alongside me. The door opened and I saw to my dismay the face of old Bushy Eyebrows was staring out at me, his face full of merriment as ever. 'Get in, Mr Hawke. You have an appointment in London.'

I knew it would be pointless to refuse and so, like an obedient little lamb, I stepped inside the sedan. Once I was seated, it drove off at speed. I guessed that I was now due for what they had called my 'debriefing' – a detailed verbal account of all that had happened to me since I had been contacted by the unfortunate Mrs Frances Clements. I was content to oblige. I had no secrets to hold. I hoped that once this was over, I would be left alone to carry on with my somewhat mundane life, unhindered by sour-faced men of sinister demeanour.

I was taken to an anonymous office block south of the river and hustled into a darkened room. I was accompanied by Bushy Eyebrows, who was joined by the thin, mealy-mouthed fellow who had visited me in hospital and had consigned the microfilm to flames. Apart from them, the other occupant of the room, who was already seated at a long desk, was a grey-haired genial looking man dressed in a neat, well-cut tweed suit and smoking a pipe. He looked more like a farmer on holiday than a high ranking member of this secret organisation, which I assumed he was.

My two escorts sat either side of this fellow like two stiff bookends. He looked up from some papers he had been studying and smiled at me. 'Ah, Mr Hawke, how lovely to see you. I hope you are fully recovered from your recent exertions....'

I was not sure how to respond to this affected cheeriness, so I just nodded.

'Good, good.' The smile broadened. 'I've just been studying your file. Most interesting.'

'I wasn't aware that I had a file.'

'Really. That is somewhat naïve of you, isn't it?' He held up a sheaf of papers. 'It's all here, from you joining into the police force in 1938 and then your enlistment in the army at the outbreak of war in 1939, to your unfortunate accident on the rifle range and your return to civvy street as a private detective, and all your exploits thereafter.' He dropped the papers on the desk. 'We like to keep a close eye on loose cannons,' he added, the genial demeanour still intact.

'When are they making the movie?'

He tapped the sheaf of papers. 'Says also that you have a dry sense of humour.'

'You've no doubt got my inside leg measurement and hat size also.'

'As a matter of fact, we have.'

And I believed him.

'So Mr Hawke… or may I call you Johnny?'

'Be my guest. As I see it, I have no control over our relationship.'

He gave me another of his avuncular smiles, not rising to the bait. 'Thank you. I am not at liberty to reveal my name I'm afraid, but you can refer to me as Socrates. Rather grand, I know, but there you are. So, Johnny,' he continued affably, 'the purpose of our meeting is for you to recount in detail, however small or insignificant it may seem to you, all that occurred, from the moment you were visited by Mrs Frances Clements employing you find her errant husband, to your unfortunate dip into the English channel. Please speak clearly. We are recording this for posterity.'

Mealy Mouth moved to what I assumed was a recording machine at the rear of the room.

I gave a shrug. 'His Master's Voice, eh?'

'In a manner of speaking,' said Socrates. 'Are you ready?'

'OK,' I said with a strong note of resignation in my voice.

And so I began my recital. I had to stop twice for them to change recording tape but I gave them what they wanted. It was no skin off my nose and it certainly did not incriminate me in any way.

When I'd finished, there was a prolonged silence in the room. Nobody spoke for at least a minute, and then Socrates leaned forward in his chair. 'That was quite excellent. Most useful. I am grateful for your cooperation.' Then he turned to his bookend companions. 'I think your job here is done, gentlemen. You may leave us.'

Both men looked disconcerted at this announcement and for some time they did not move. Bushy Eyebrows, in particular, looked angry at this brusque dismissal.

Socrates waved a hand gently like a dying butterfly. 'As I intimated, you can go now, gentlemen,' he added with emphasis.

Reluctantly, like angry sleepwalkers, the two men left the room.

'Ah, there's always someone who doesn't know when it's time to leave the party. Charming fellows in their own way,' said Socrates, 'good at their job and all that. They just lack a touch of humanity and, dare I say, vision.'

'I am sure you can say whatever you like. It's obvious that you're the big cheese around here.'

He laughed out loud. 'A dry sense of humour indeed. Perhaps I ought to call myself Big Cheese instead of Socrates.'

'Can I go now? I'd quite like to leave the party, too.'

'Presently, Johnny. There are one or two things I want to say to you; one or two things I want to clear up.'

'I'm afraid you've squeezed all the juice out of me. I assure you I've told you all I know.'

'All you know, maybe, but not necessarily all you think.'

'I don't know what are you talking about?'

'The girl. Susan. She is our main concern now. She is a key link to the big boys in the Ruskie organisation and we need to get hold of her. Apart from anything else, she's wanted for a double murder.'

'A double murder?'

Socrates nodded. 'You saw her shoot Brewer, the boat owner,

but it is most likely that she was responsible for his crony's death also. The Aurora was found drifting in the Channel with no one aboard'. He gave a bleak smile. 'Like a junior Marie Celeste. It's most likely the girl cut the boat adrift and disposed of the two bodies in the sea. But, more importantly than that, it is obvious she is one of their top agents and, as such, has much information that would be of great assistance to us. Anything at all that you can tell me about her would be most useful.'

'Like what? She was just a pretty girl in her late twenties, as I told you, but with a streak running through her as cold and as hard as steel. Strong, intelligent, pretty face. Well educated, I should say.'

'Accent?'

I thought for a moment. 'She didn't have one – not a strong one anyway. Bordering on the posh, I suppose. Just well-spoken English.'

'Any distinguishing features?'

'None that I could see.'

Socrates smiled. 'So you didn't get that close.'

'I didn't. She was a fair actress, for she convinced me in her role of Clements' distressed sister. Apparently, she could turn on the emotions and tears at will.'

'Have you any idea where she might be now?'

'Of course not. If I did, I'd wring her neck.'

'In that case, I'm glad you have no notion of her whereabouts. She is more useful to us alive.'

I shrugged. 'Just an expression. Homicide is not my line. May I go now?'

Socrates held up his forefinger to halt my action of rising from my chair. 'You are a very likely lad, Mr Hawke. In this affair, you've shown courage, tenacity and ingenuity. The service could use fellows like you. Might you be persuaded to join us?'

'The secret service?'

Socrates frowned. 'We never call ourselves that. This organisation has many rooms, many departments. The secret service is only a term used in cheap fiction. We are all national security operatives, and we serve one aim.'

'Which is?'

'The security of the British isles. You tried to serve your country once and were prevented from doing so by that unfortunate accident. Perhaps now you'd like to have another go.'

'I'm flattered by the offer, but I'm afraid that I'm not much of a team player. I reckon the last thing you want is a rogue operative. I tend to follow my own path. I'd feel hemmed in by so rules and restrictions. As a private detective, I have no one to answer to but myself – and that's the way I like it. Sorry.'

Socrates nodded sagely. 'So am I. It is a pity, but I understand. I suspect part of your success and survival rests on your ability to be a free spirit.'

'I have never really thought about it in that way, but you could be right.'

'Well, if you change your mind…' He reached into his waistcoat pocket and produced a card. 'This is my private number. Just issue the password 'Charlemagne' and you'll be put straight through to me.'

I took the card and slipped it into my wallet. 'So, if that is all, can I really go home now?'

Socrates nodded and his hand hovered over the telephone. 'I'll arrange for a car to take you there.'

CHAPTER THIRTY THREE
From the journal of Johnny Hawke

It was strange entering my old office after such a long absence. It was just as I remembered it but with an extra layer of dust that, with the dim light filtering through the grimy windows, added an extra greyness to the ambience. Even when I switched on the light, the place had a kind of sepulchral gloom. It was like the Johnny Hawke museum, I mused. There was a scattering of post on the floor which on a quick examination told me that none of the messages were from desperate potential clients offering me exorbitant fees to find their beloved pussycat. It was just a collection of bills and a government circular. I wandered to my back room, made myself a cup of black coffee and returned to sit in my office chair. Then, I smiled. It was good to be home. It was good to get back to normality. It was good to return to my old familiar life. I felt my body relax for the first time in weeks, and as it did so, it also alerted me to the fact that I was actually very hungry. Well, with a grin materialising, I knew what to do about that.

As I made my way to Benny's café, I was aware that the old boy would bombard me with questions regarding my absence and what had happened to the girl Susan. I had no intention of telling him the truth. I would never hear the end of it and besides, it was a security matter. I didn't want Bushy Eyebrows to come knocking again claiming I was a risk to the nation's safety because I'd blabbed to a little Jewish café owner. By the time I had arrived, I had managed to concoct a convincing cock and bull story to satisfy the old boy and get him off my back.

It was late afternoon when I stepped across the threshold of my favoured eating establishment. It was a quiet time in the rhythm of the café's day. The luncheon crew had gone and it was too early for the tea time rush. The place was empty. At the sound of the tinkling doorbell, Benny emerged from the kitchen and on seeing me, he let out a whelp of joy and ran forward, throwing his arms around me.

'Johnny, Johnny, my boy. Thank heavens. Where have you been? I have been worried sick about you. Are you all right?'

Disentangling myself from his embrace, I smiled at the old boy. 'I'm fine. And I'm hungry.'

'Of course, of course. I'll rustle up some grub for you but first, you must tell me where you've been. Where's that lovely girl Susan? What has happened?'

I shook my head, the smile still painted on my mug. 'Nothing has happened. The case fizzled out. Simple as that. We hit a dead end, so she went back to Brighton and I stayed down there for a week or two – a kind of holiday.'

'With her?'

I shook my head. 'No, no. Nothing like that. She has a fiancé. You are always constructing romances for me, Benny. She was a client, that's all.'

'Well, you could have let me know where you were. You know how I worry about you. Brighton, eh? Not even a postcard.'

I patted him gently on the back. 'I know. I'm sorry. I'm a bit of a thoughtless bastard at times.'

'That you are. But it's good to see the thoughtless bastard has returned – but you look pale and thinner.'

'Food in Brighton is not as good as yours.'

His eyes twinkled. 'Of course not. OK, sit down and I'll bring you today's special: meat and potato pie. Sadly, not so much meat and a lot of potato, I'm afraid. This rationing – it will close me down.' With a characteristic shrug of the shoulders, he returned to the kitchen.

I sat at my usual table, relieved that Benny had accepted my lies. Apart from anything else, I didn't want to recount my exploits all over again. They're on tape now locked in a vault somewhere in Whitehall.

As I settled down to devour my meal, Benny sat by me, cradling a hot mug of tea his hands. 'Good grub, eh, Johnny?'

Mouth full, I nodded. In truth, it was pleasant enough but the thin slivers of beef hidden in the pie were few and far between. Nevertheless, the concoction filled my tummy and gave me a feeling of wellbeing. Pushing my empty plate away, I lit up a cigarette.

'Thanks, Benny. It's good to be back,' I said and meant it.

'So, what are you going to do with the lady's things? The stuff she left behind.'

I paused, unsure what Benny had just said. 'What stuff?' I asked, as I felt my body stiffening.

'Some of her clothes and her case. Those things she left behind when you raced off together. Surely you'll want to return them to her.'

'Show me,' I cried, jumping up from my seat.

'Sure, but aren't you going to let your food settle first?'

'I'm fine. Just let me see Susan's stuff.'

'They're in the spare room...'

'I know where that is. I'll just check it out. How about you make me another pot of tea?'

Benny's face creased in puzzlement at my sudden urgent need to see Susan's things. He couldn't know that I thought that maybe they may provide some clue as to her whereabouts – some means of tracking the traitorous hussy down.

I hared up the stairs to the spare room. It was neat and tidy with some of her clothes on the bed – a couple of jumpers, a blouse, and a skirt. There were items of makeup on the dressing table and a suitcase by the wardrobe. There was nothing in the chest of drawers apart from a couple of crusty old mothballs. I examined the clothes and makeup, but there was nothing there that could give me any clue to help me locate my darling Susan. The labels were all from ordinary high street stores that could be found in any town in Britain. The wardrobe was also empty, as was the case. It seemed she had been scrupulous in making sure there was nothing incriminating left behind.

I sat on the bed, dismayed and frustrated. My eyes wandered around the room looking for something, just something; but there was nothing. Then, my gaze landed back on the suitcase. I had already checked it out thoroughly, even ripped open the lining, but the search had proved fruitless. Then, I noticed the luggage label attached to the handle. This had escaped my scrutiny. I bent down and looked at it closely. The label had an address located in Brighton. No doubt a false one to support her claim that she lived there as the sister of Frances Clements. However, on instinct, I scratched away the paper label and, lo and behold, there was a second label underneath, featuring another address in faded writing. Could this be a genuine one? The girl's real address? One could only hope. And I did.

I lifted the label from its moorings and slipped it into my pocket. It was the feeblest of straws, but I was happy to grasp it.

CHAPTER THIRTY FOUR
From the journal of Johnny Hawke

The faded writing on the luggage label led me to a smart block
of flats in Chelsea: Melville Mansions. The apartment that I was
interested in, according to the label I had unearthed, was Flat
3B. A uniformed commissionaire on sentry duty outside the
building stationed by the revolving door cast a wary
disapproving eye over me as I approached. He no doubt thought
this scruffy individual in a shabby raincoat and battered trilby
had no business in sullying his golden portal, but I suspected
discretion prevented him from barring my way. After all, I could
be an eccentric millionaire. I tipped the brim of my hat as I
passed by him and gave him a gladsome smile. He remained
poker-faced.

I checked the names of the inhabitants of this swanky
residence on the noticeboard in the foyer. Flat 3B was registered
as being occupied by Miss Elsa Smith. Fingers crossed, she
must be my old lady friend Susan Kershaw. Flat 3B was located
on the first floor, so I made my way up there via the lift without
delay. I pressed the doorbell but I could hear no tintinnabulation
within. Perhaps the bell was broken or located so deep inside
the flat that the sound didn't make it to the outer reaches. Plan
B: I knocked hard on the door.

Almost as a Pavlovian response, the door of the adjoining flat
flew open, and what appeared to be a pantomime dame stuck
her head out. Well, it was a lady of considerably advanced years
whose face was caked in pale pink powder, lips inexpertly
adorned with garish red lipstick and the eyes smeared with
aquamarine eye shadow. This grotesque image was completed
by an ill-fitting blonde wig which looked as though it had been
borrowed from a scarecrow.

'She's moved out,' this creature affirmed in a buzz saw of a
voice. 'Gone away. Some weeks now.'

'Ah, I see.'

'So there's no use you trying to get an answer.' This was said in such a way that it was quite clear that it was a prompt for me to be on my way. She didn't want any scruffy individuals banging on doors next to her exclusive apartment.

'Do you know where she has gone?' I asked sweetly. I may be scruffy, but I maintained my pleasant demeanour.

'Of course not. We keep ourselves to ourselves in Melville Mansions,' came the brusque reply.

I could see from her stern expression and that gorgon stare that she had no intention of closing her door until I had removed myself from her sight.

I touched my hat again in a gentlemanly fashion, said 'Thank you and good day,' and made my way back to the lift. She watched me every inch of the way. Stepping in the lift, I turned and gave her a wave. She gave a snort of indignation and slammed her door. In an instant, I was out of the lift and had returned to apartment 3B. Burgling kit at the ready, working as quietly as I could so as not to alert Widow Twankey next door, I affected an entry.

It was a plush pad indeed. Certainly in a different league to the environs of Hawke Towers, with its clean, modern and expensive furniture and rich exotic drapes, but it was devoid of character and any sense that someone lived here. I soon discovered that this was partly due to the fact that Elsa Smith had taken all her personal belongings with her. She had stripped the place of her personality. I did a minute search of the place but the cupboard was bare. Not a tin of beans, a dirty ashtray or a discarded newspaper was to be found. Even when I dropped down to gaze under the bed, hoping there might be something there, it appeared that even the fluff had been removed. It looked like I had reached a dead end. What on earth was I to do now?

My cogitations were interrupted by a sound from the hallway. I stood still and waited, wishing I'd brought my gun. But then, all was silence. Cautiously I moved towards the hall and peered around the door. There on the doormat was a long white envelope which hadn't been there when I arrived. Could it have come from the harridan next door informing me that she knew I had made an illegal entry and had phoned the police? As I picked up the envelope I saw that it bore a stamp. Of course, the postman had come to call. The noise I had heard was the letterbox flap and the envelope dropping on the mat.

My knowledge of philately is close to nil but I could tell that the stamp was of foreign origin and the airmail sticker in the top left-hand corner easily confirmed this. The letter was addressed to my friend Miss Elsa Smith. As she wasn't around to open it, I decided to take the liberty. There was a foolscap sheet of quality paper within which bore a rather grand looking letter heading from a foreign firm which I worked out were probably house agents and based in Amsterdam. The correspondence was dated three weeks earlier, suggesting that this missive had been lost in the post. Thankfully, the text of the letter was in English and addressed to 'Dear Miss Elsa Smith'. What followed thrilled me to the core. It seemed that I had hit the jackpot. The contents of this correspondence was confirmation that the arrangements were settled for Miss Smith to take possession of a small house in the Jordaan district of Amsterdam. There was even the address. So, 14 Rozenstratt was her new bolthole. She had left the old country for pastures new because things were getting a little hot for her. She had moved to the land of clogs and tulips. I laughed out loud. 'You can run, my dear Elsa stroke Susan, but I'll catch up with thee ere long,' I cried.

CHAPTER THIRTY FIVE
From the journal of Johnny Hawke

Although I have only been up in an aeroplane a few times in my life, I am not a fan of flying. Neither is my stomach. I am afraid I am a member of that clan who believes that if men were meant to fly, we'd have been given feathers and wings and probably a beak. In truth, it isn't the actual flying that gives me the collywobbles; it is the taking off and landing. For the former, I have trouble in conceiving how a large lump of metal is able to propel its bulky form up from the ground and into the clouds and still remain airborne; with the latter it's the bumping, shuddering of the plane as it hits the tarmac, screeching like a distressed child as it grinds to a halt. As I walked across the tarmac at London Airport towards the shiny BEA Silver Wing crouching there, I felt my stomach muscles tighten with apprehension. Having faced many dangerous life-threatening situations in my life, I do not regard myself a coward, but where flying is concerned, I am a realist!

Once we were airborne, I was supplied with a large gin and tonic by a pretty stewardess and this helped me relax. I downed another just before we landed at Schiphol Airport. The customs procedure was thorough, as it had been in London. My money allowance was checked, as was my small suitcase, with my socks and underwear held up for scrutiny. I had been wise enough not to try and smuggle my revolver, for not only would it have been found but no doubt I would have been held for questioning and possibly arrested. The lack of a weapon disadvantaged me in my mission but that could not be helped.

Eventually, I followed the stream of passengers heading for the bus depot to board a coach to take us into the centre of Amsterdam. An hour later, I was standing by the stately structure of the city's railway station where the coach had dropped me along with a swathe of fellow passengers.

Now, things were about to get serious. I was nearing the end of my mission, Operation Elsa. As usual, I had no firm plan of action in mind, I just trusted my natural instincts, hoping they would see me through. The only person I had told of my trip to Amsterdam and the purpose behind it was David Llewellyn. I knew if I had told Socrates, he would have stopped me. This was my affair, something I had to do myself and I didn't want anyone to step in and prevent me. David had put me in touch with Albert Van Doran, a colleague in the Amsterdam Police Department, and this Dutch policeman had assured me that his department would provide me with full assistance when the time was ripe. A telephone call was all that would be needed.

I hailed a taxi and gave him the details of my destination: 14 Rozenstraatt in the Jordaan district.

It was a handsome little house, tall and narrow with a bright red door, situated on a quiet pedestrianised street. There were tubs of coloured flowers outside and variegated ivy straggled up the wall. It was the picture of calm, neat domesticity. I had no intention of utilising the large brass knocker to announce my arrival and so, in my time-honoured fashion, I affected an entry.

I waited in the narrow hallway and listened for any sounds which would indicate that the lady was in residence. There were none. I moved into the sitting room. It was delightfully appointed with modern furniture: spiky legged chairs, a large curvy sofa, a stylish sideboard in light wood, three large stoneware based lamps and a red fleecy rug. It looked like one of those pictures you were likely to find in a magazine which dealt with smart, up-to-date décor. Thinking of my own tatty quarters, I was jealous. The spy game must pay well.

I was delighted to see a bright shiny telephone on a small coffee table in close proximity to the sofa. I gazed around me intently, looking for signs, clues that I had come to the right place and this indeed was the dwelling of Elsa Smith aka Susan Kershaw. One thing that caught my eyes was a framed photograph in pride of place on the tiled mantelpiece. I picked it up and examined it. There were two smiling figures staring out at me. One was my darling Susan or Elsa, as I should think of her now. Well, that confirmed I had come to the right place.

In the photograph, she was leaning affectionately on the shoulder of an older man. With a minor electric shock up my spine, I realised I recognised him. It was a famous face.

Scrawled at the bottom of the photograph in elegant handwriting were the words, 'Love from Daddy.' In an instant, my brain began whirling trying to click certain pieces into place. Could the scenario that was forming in my mind be really the truth? Had I uncovered a terrible secret?

While I was mulling this over, I heard the front door open. This was it, then.

Within seconds Elsa Smith, my old buddy who I had known as Susan Kershaw, entered the room. Her hair was shorter now and dyed black, but the face was still as pretty. On seeing me standing by the fireplace, she froze, her features held in a state of shock.

'You!' she said.

'Yes, little me.'

'What… what are you doing here?' The words came out before she realised the stupidity of them and her face registered she recognised the fact.

'I've come for you.'

'What the hell do you mean?'

'You're going back lady to, as they say, face the music.'

She laughed. I could not be sure if it was genuine or theatrical.

'And how do you propose to take me back?'

'I am sure the Netherlands authorities will be most happy to arrange for the deportation of a British spy. I only have to make a phone call.'

'How did you find me?'

'I have my methods. I am a private detective after all, although I suspect you underestimated my prowess.'

She smiled. 'A little, I suppose.'

'Your new hairstyle suits you.'

'You've lost weight.'

'Being in the sea for some time and nearly drowning does have that effect.'

'Let's have a drink,' she said, moving easily to the drinks trolley. 'Scotch for you, I suspect.'

'That will be fine. How long have you worked for the Russians?'

'Ah, the interrogation begins.' She handed me a tumbler with a generous slug of whisky. I took it but I had no intention of drinking any of it. I did not trust this sexy but very slippery customer an inch. I could not forget that she had tried to kill me once already. 'Perhaps a more pertinent question would be: why do you work for the Russians?'

'Oh, why? That is easy. Britain is going down the drain. It's a corrupt, stratified, capitalist society. Soviet Communism is the only secure political system and the best defence against the rise of fascism. In Britain, we have an elite government and the social dichotomy of the haves and have nots. Communism provides a system of social organization in which all property is owned by the community and each person contributes and receives according to their ability and needs.'

I held up my hand. 'Spare me the lecture,' I barked. 'It's water off a duck's back to me. Bleak ideologies that ignore humanity make me want to puke. Regimes without humanity...' My anger got the better of me and I ran out of words. 'You turned your back on your own country to meddle with Commie bastards, no doubt indoctrinated by your daddy.'

Instinctively, Elsa glanced at the photograph on the mantelpiece. 'What do you know about my father?' she cried.

'Enough. That photo tells all, doesn't it?'

'You bastard. You interfering bastard!' With a swift motion, she dropped down into a crouch and from her handbag, pulled out a small pistol and aimed it at me. Here we go again. Déjà vu time. I flung myself sideways and dropped to the floor. The bullet hit one of the stoneware lamps, which shattered, spraying splinters of pottery in all directions.

Elsa now headed for the door, but before I could get to my feet, she turned and fired again. This time, her aim was more accurate. I felt a searing pain in my left shoulder and dropped down on the carpet with a groan. After a moment, with gritted teeth and a subdued whelp of pain, I struggled to my feet. I heard the front door slam shut. She was getting away; I was not about to let this happen. Despite my throbbing shoulder, I galvanised myself into action and raced after her. Once out on the street, I saw her heading up towards the main road. Ignoring the pain of my wound, I upped my game, forcing my legs into top gear and pounded the pavement in pursuit. Gradually, I began to gain on her.

Just as she reached the main road which ran along the canal-side, she instinctively turned round to check on my progress. It was obvious from her expression that she was shocked, not only that I was up and running, but that I was catching up to her. In a frantic action, she raised her gun and fired at me again, but she was too distracted now and the shot went wild. I was near enough to her to see the fear and panic in her face. In desperation, she turned and, without looking, ran into the road directly into the path of a delivery van. There was a dull thump as her body connected with the bonnet of the vehicle. The impact caused her to be thrown forward some six feet into the air before crashing down on the cobbles. For a brief moment, the world froze and became like a still photograph. No one or nothing moved and suddenly, as though some ethereal film director had issued the instruction 'action', there was an immediate flurry of activity. Pedestrians seemed to appear from nowhere. The van driver and other motorists emerged from their vehicles to gather around Elsa's body. I heard the van driver shouting, 'She just ran out in front of me. I hadn't a chance…'

When I reached the scene, someone was saying, 'We must ring for an ambulance,' but I could see that it was too late for that. A hearse would be more appropriate. Elsa lay in the dust of the road, her head cradled by the curb. Her neck was twisted awkwardly and a thin trail of blood was trickling from her mouth. Her eyes, those strong grey eyes, were open, staring sightlessly heavenwards.

I could not help but feel a certain sadness at the sight, but I consoled myself with the thought that she was a traitor, and had suffered a traitor's death.

CHAPTER THIRTY SIX
From the journal of Johnny Hawke

I had never been to the Athenaeum Club before, although I had passed it many times whenever my travails around London had taken me down Pall Mall. As Benny might well have observed, it was not a place for commoners like us. It was where posh, privileged people gathered and noshed. He was probably right, but on this occasion, as I approached the Doric portico of this illustrious building, I knew I would be granted entry because I had been invited there. This was in response to a phone call I had made to Socrates requesting a meeting. He was more than happy to oblige and was most intrigued to learn what I had to tell him. He had suggested lunch at his club, the Athenaeum. Who was I to disagree?

On entering this hallowed building, I gave my name to the flunkey at the desk. He checked the register and it seemed I was expected. Another flunkey was summoned and he divested me of my hat and coat, apparently struggling not to sneer at their market stall quality. I was then delivered to the dining room, which for some reason is called the Coffee Room. No doubt to confuse interlopers like me.

The room had the air of a public library. The few diners that were there spoke in soft voices and wore serious, studious expressions. Socrates, whose real name I still did not know, was seated by the far wall in front of a bookcase which displayed a fine array of ancient volumes. He saw me as I entered, half rose from his chair and beckoned me forward with the wave of his hand.

'Good to see you, John,' he said cheerfully, proffering his hand. I took it and shook it. It was as though I was having lunch with a jovial uncle rather than some kind of government spymaster. He raised a bottle of wine from a silver cooler and poured me a glass. 'You must try this Sauterne, it's an 1855 vintage, quite one of the best.'

I nodded and took a sip. Well, it seemed OK, but my

uneducated tongue told me no more. I am afraid to me it didn't taste much different from the *vin ordinaire* that I sometimes treated myself to at the local off licence when I was in funds. No wonder I'm not a member of this club. Benny is right, I am a common fellow.

Socrates passed me the menu, a single stiff card with elegant curlicue writing. The prices were eye-watering. How different from Benny's handwritten sheet of foolscap. The letters swam before my eyes. I could see that there was no mention of pie and mash.

'I recommend the celeriac soup followed by the turbot. Certainly avoid the veal. It tends to be overcooked.'

'I'll take your advice,' I said softly.

'So, how is the shoulder?'

I raised a quizzical brow. 'You know?'

He smiled, which just bordered on the patronising. 'Of course, dear boy. Once someone falls under our scrutiny, they never leave it. You are now permanently on our radar. '

'If that is the case, you also know about Elsa.'

He nodded, his features clouding briefly. 'Oh, yes. We know that she is dead and that you have been a bit of a pain in the nether regions. You really should have told us about it. A solo excursion to Amsterdam to beard the lady in her new Dutch quarters was very reckless and foolhardy. You have lost us a valuable source of information.'

'If you could have caught her. She wasn't going to give up easily. I am not sure that she didn't deliberately run in front of that van to escape capture. There is no guarantee your boys could have been more successful than I.'

Socrates paused and took a sip of wine. 'I believe you have a point,' he said. 'It is distressing nonetheless. But... your shoulder. It has healed?'

'Yes. I'm fine now. It was, as they say in the westerns, "just a scratch."'

'I'm pleased to hear it.'

At that moment, a waiter appeared by our table. So silent and discreet had been his approach that he gave the impression of having materialised out of thin air. Socrates gave him our order and he quickly melted into the background once more.

'Now then, John, you told me on the telephone that you have some information to pass on that will be of great interest to us.'

'I do. Tell me, what do you know of Elsa's history?'

'Ah, there you have us. Our investigations have failed to discover anything definite about her background or how she became entangled with the Communists. In fact, she only came under our scrutiny because of this affair. Ironically, it was her involvement with you that brought her to our attention.'

'You will then be surprised to learn who her father was.'

'Undoubtedly...' The reply came slowly, his eyes flickering with renewed interest.

I took the photograph from my jacket pocket and passed it to him. 'A present from Amsterdam,' I said.

He scrutinised the photograph for a few moments, his features registering no emotion whatsoever.

'Isn't that...?' I proffered.

He held up his hand to prevent me from using the name.

'It is. That is certain.' He slipped the photograph into his coat pocket. 'That is most useful. I thank you for this, John. It makes up immeasurably for the loss of Elsa.'

'My pleasure.'

'Ah, here comes our soup. *Bon appetit.*'

There was no more talk of the photograph or the man who appeared in it, and the meal was eaten with little conversation. It was as though the business of the day had already been concluded and there was nothing more left to say.

Socrates consumed little of his main course, picking idly at the fish. After he had finished eating, he pushed his plate gently to one side and said, 'Do order a pudding along with brandy and coffee, if you so wish. It's all paid for, dear boy, but I have to leave you now. Pressing business and all that.' Without waiting for a reply, he dropped his napkin on to his plate, rose from the table and moved around to my chair. Leaning close to my ear, he spoke softly to me. 'Mum's the word about the photo you understand.'

I nodded.

'Good man. And remember, the offer is still open. If you

would like to join us to fight the good fight, you would be very welcome.'

With that, he was gone, striding across the plush carpet towards the door.

I stayed and had a pudding with a coffee and brandy. Why not? It wasn't every day that I could dine in such style. I would never say it to Benny, of course, but it was rather better than the fare that he was able to supply. I looked at my empty dish and swigged my brandy. *Ah*, I thought, *I don't think the Athenaeum had heard of rationing*.

CHAPTER THIRTY SEVEN
From the journal of Johnny Hawke

About a week after my slap-up lunch at the Athenaeum, I was back in the old harness in the detective business. I had a client. Whoopee! It was certainly a climb down from the dizzy heights of murder and espionage. It was only a matter of suspected adultery – but the air of normality that this brought was rather comforting. Peering through keyholes, trailing suspected illicit couples and hanging about the damp streets was hardly exciting or fulfilling work, but it was much less dangerous than being shot at or dumped in the sea. In this new case, my client was the husband who suspected his wife of playing away and he was prepared to pay well to be proved right. He was, he told me, desperate to find evidence of her treachery so he could 'dump the old tart.' Each to his own, I suppose.

Happy to be back in the old routine and flush in funds again, I decided to treat myself to a pint of bitter and a bag of crisps at the Horse and Trumpet at lunchtime. Hardly in the same league as the Athenaeum but, if the truth be told, more my barrow.

As I sat hunched up at the bar on a tall stool, sipping my pint and crunching my crisps, I felt a strange kind satisfied ease settle on me. My whole body relaxed and I smiled. Absentmindedly, I reached out and picked up a daily paper that someone had left behind on the counter. It was the *Daily Telegraph.* Immediately, the headline and accompanying photograph caught my attention. The story was related to the arrest of a respected titled diplomat working for the Foreign Office on suspicion of spying for the Russians. I gazed at the grey-faced bowler hatted-gentleman who stared out at me from the front page of the newspaper. I recognised that face as I had done so before in a certain photograph. So, they'd caught up with Elsa's daddy at last. I drained my glass and ordered another pint.

EPILOGUE

It was a dull, misty morning when two black saloon cars drew up outside the building which housed the offices of Klenco. Stepping out of the first car were two men. One, wearing a tweed overcoat, had large staring eyes and bushy eyebrows. The other, dressed in a grey gabardine raincoat, was a thin fellow, with gaunt features and a small, mean mouth. They were joined by the occupants of the second car, three burly men, also dressed in grey raincoats.

The man in the tweed coat gave a decisive nod to the others and then led the way into the building.

Roland Sanders was about to light up a small cigar when he heard loud noises from the outer office and then the scream of his secretary. Before he could move, the door burst open and two men entered; Bushy Eyebrows and his grey-faced associate.

'What is the meaning of this intrusion?' snapped Sanders.

'We've come to take you away, Roland.'

'If you don't get out of here, I'll call the authorities.'

The man smiled. It wasn't a pleasant smile. 'We're already here. We are the authorities, Roland.'

Now Sanders' anger turned to disquiet while on its way to naked fear. 'There must be some mistake. What are you talking about?' he croaked. Although at the back of his mind, he had a stomach-churning suspicion he knew exactly what they were talking about.

'You've involved yourself with activities detrimental to the safety of this sceptred isle, Roland. You know what I mean. We've come to take you into custody. Now it's time to pay for your misdemeanours.'

'I don't know what you mean.'

Bushy Eyebrows turned to his colleague. 'I expected our friend here to be brighter than this. In simple terms, Roland, the game is up. We know all about your involvement with the Russian circuit. Sir Jeremy has told us all about you. After we applied a little persuasive pressure, that is.' Suddenly, Bushy

Eyebrows produced a gun from his overcoat pocket. 'I do hope you are going to come with us without any fuss. In one sense, I would hate to use this, but in another, it would give me great pleasure to shoot a dirty traitor.'

'No, don't shoot. I'll come with you, of course…'

'Sensible man. In this instance, at least.'

They passed through the outer office where the other men were waiting. Sanders' secretary stood trembling by the filing cabinet, shaking with fear. She had no idea what was going on, who these men were and what they wanted with her boss. Strangely, in seconds, they had all trailed out of the office, along with Mr Sanders, who was ashen of face and looked close tears. They closed the door behind them.

Printed in Great Britain
by Amazon